The
826
Quarterly

An 826 Valencia original

Published Summer 2006,
as the sixth edition of the 826 Quarterly.
Created by all hands on deck at 826 Valencia.
www.826valencia.org

Special editorial attention was provided by
Keren Ackerman, Dave Adams, Lisa Amick, Sona Avakian,
Rachel Chalmer, Joe Conway, Kathryn Crim, Veronica Dakota,
Tom Edwards, Lara Fox, Ellen Goodenow, Lauren Hall, Mike Harkin,
Nalani Jay, Suzanne Klein, Kevin Klein, Mimi Lok, Belinda Man,
Abner Morales, Rosey Rouhana, Nora Salim, Karen Wagstaffe,
James Warner, Elka Weber, Dan Weiss, Eric Willinski, Miranda Yaver

Book design and production by Chloë Greene,
Ashley Neese, Alvaro Villanueva.

ISBN: 0-9790073-0-5
978-0-9790073-0-9

Printed in Canada by WestCan P.G.

The
826
Quarterly

[Published twice yearly at least]

VOLUME 6 • SUMMER 2006

This volume of the 826 Quarterly
is dedicated to Mr. Blue, our publisher,
because he said so (and still gave us his
disapproving scowl when we did).

Contents

Foreword . . . . *by Erika Lopez*   xii

**The Staff, Board, Interns, and Volunteers
of 826 Valencia**   xv

826 Valencia Programs Overview   xxiv

826 National   xxix

I. WORKSHOPS

Change the Past to Change the Future . . . . . . *by Akeya Harris*   3

The Case of the Sparkly
    Pink Hello Kitty Pen . . . . *by Emily Mayer*   10

Flowers in Her Hair . . . . *by Emily Mayer*   12

Robby's Poem . . . . *by Robby Stosick*   14

About Mariah Carey . . . . *by Brendan Sasso*   15

Boring Paragraph . . . . *by Claire Williams*   16

The Throbbing Arm
    and the Spinning Ballroom . . . . *by Phoebe Morgan
                                                        & Siobhan Willing*   17

My Great Dinner Party . . . . *by Corinna Tam*   19

My Great Dinner Party; Caution: Rated "R" . . . *by Elliot Tam*   20

Good Cajun Daughter . . . . *by Roz LaBean*   21

Girl Story . . . . *by Esher Jones Esteves*   22

Book's Letter . . . . *by Peerapat Teerawattanasook*   23

The Daily Phone Call from Mom . . . . *by Vicky Guan*   25

Think About What You Do . . . . *by Philip Nguy*   27

Fire . . . . *by Devon Kearney*   28

Dragon's Charm .... *by Devon Kearney* 29

Flying Through the Pieces of My Heart ... *by Devon Kearney* 30

Ranger Ranger Turns
    into a Bad Tangerine .... *by Emma Hyndman* 31

The Mystery of the Tangerine Forest .... *by Aly Robalino* 33

A Hat .... *by Sabine Dahi* 41

Sound .... *by Maya Chatterjee* 42

It is a Tree .... *by Chris Danison* 43

Magic Box .... *by Maya Chatterjee* 44

Mystery Figure .... *by Chris Danison* 45

Monarch Butterfly .... *by Casey Roos* 46

My Driving Lessons .... *by Ray Perez* 47

Thai Quest .... *by Tien Ortman* 52

Everett Celebrates Day of Peace .... *by Karla Hernandez* 55

The Secret of Blockbuster Hits .... *by Guillermo Gonzalez* 56

III. AT-LARGE SUBMISSIONS

Flashbulb .... *by Christina Jones* 61

Faking It .... *by Liz Benefiel* 65

Unbearable Pain .... *by John Fernandez* 72

Douglass Keith LaBean I .... *by Roz LaBean* 74

Clouds I .... *by Austin Lewis* 77

My Yellow .... *by Stormy Kelly* 78

Yellow Wall .... *by Jasmin Rivera* 80

Auntie E. .... *by Vaosa Logovii* 81

The Man with the Straight Face .... *by Ana Enciso* 83

Obituary in Three Drafts .... *by Teresa Cotsirilos* 86

Chaparrito Pero Picoso . . . . *by Fredy Coronado*   91

Escape   . . . . *by Jessica Balidio*   93

Never Close Your Eyes . . . . *by Gina Cargas*   95

Sapiens Kingdom . . . . *by Max Marttila*   99

Quiet . . . . *by Hua Ling Zhao*   108

Boy Up a Tree . . . . *by Elizabeth Neveu*   109

Pink . . . . *by Daniel Abuella*   99

You Bring the Muy Caliente Outta Me . . . . *by Mayra Recinos*   116

Insomnia . . . . *by Joanna Amick*   118

Piratehood Explained . . . . *by Layla Durrani*   120

The Store at 826 Valencia   122

FOREWORD

BY MRS. LOPEZ

The Buccaneers at **826 VALENCIA** have made a sort of an artistic family for those of us who're used to being excused from the dinner table for being "INAPPROPRIATE."

Before visiting 826 Valencia, I didn't even think I liked kids all that much. Sure, I liked the odd hoodlum, as anyone would. But I'm mostly from the Jersey suburbs. Need I say more? Okay, it's just that you WANNA CARRY CYANIDE TABLETS in a ring for when you get too old to out run them.

BUT I've never seen so much ENTHUSIASM, curiosity, tenacity, & Heart in ONE PLACE

I'M NOT KIDDING. AND IT'S **CONTAGIOUS** I VISITED A CLASS ONE DAY and SIMPLY loved FEELING LIKE THE cynical OLD aunt in the MUUMUU who CONSTANTLY BLURTS OUT ADVICE, FOR NO REASON at ALL.

GET A RECEIPT!

But BY THE TIME I LEFT, I WAS one of THE "KIDS," and DECIDED to wear SUNGLASSES, call MYSELF a HOT SHOT PRODUCER, And turn ONE of MY OWN BOOKS INTO a movie instead of sitting AROUND ON a SATURDAY night, WAITING FOR the phone to RING.

I'VE since tossed my cyanide SPY RING and LIKE THE OLD aunt, I STILL WORRY FOR these KIDS and WANT them to call if/when they GET scared FROM TAKING on the WORLD. They gave me back a YOUNGER me, AND in **THE CREATIVE LIFE**, you **Never** get too OLD to hear:

Go ahead! Why NOT? Got anything better TO DO?

Enjoy!

Summer 2006

Connie Coady	Belinda Man
Joshua Fischel	Sally Mao
Isaac Fitzgerald	Kamala Puligandla
Daniel Gumbiner	Dan Weiss
Dustin Johnston	Miranda Yaver
Andrew Kirchner	

The Many Volunteers, Tutors, and Workshop Teachers at 826 Valencia

Keren Ackerman, Nathan Adachi, Mike Adamick, David Adams, Jonathon Adams, Miranda Adkins, Yousef Al-Balouchi, Daniel Alarcon, Alison Alkire, Pat Allbee, Max Allbee, Elise Allen, Nicki Allen, Gerald Ambinder, Mulu Amha, Lisa Amick, Christina Amini, Kyle Anderson, Lessley Anderson, Sarah Anderson, Tim Anderson, Louis Anthes, Heather Antonissen, Andrea Arata, Amity Armstrong, Jessica Arndt, Darcy Asbe, Amelia Ashton, Chris Askew, Ellen Atkinson, Amy Atkinson, David Atlas, Kirstin Ault, Sona Avakian, Michele Ayala, Evan Babb, Sally Baggett, Nisi Baier, Michael Bailey, Maria Baird, Monya Baker, Laurie Baker-Flynn, Gina Balibrera, Ariel Balter, Eric Bankston, Leticia Barajas, Nicky Batill, Kevin Bayley, Colleen Bazdaric, Neva Beach, Rebecca Beal, Maren Bean, Dana Beatty, Meg Beaudet, Devon Beddard, Rachel Been, Bonnie Begusch, David Beisly-Guiotto, Lara Belonogoff, Nicole Bender, Jennifer Bennett, Juliette Berg, Michael Berger, Debra Berliner, Kathryn Bertram, Jason Biehl, Alexei Bien, Paige Bierma, Daniel Biewener, Tim Billings, Jessica Binder, Lucinda Bingham, Alec Binnie, Jennifer Birch, Jenny Bitner, Colin Blake, Tracy Blanchard, John Blanco, Adam J. Blane, Rebecca Blatt, Joni Blecher, Summer Block, Michael Blossom, Steve Blumenthal, Tamara Bock, Charles Boodman, Kelly Booth, Matthew Borden, John Borland, Linda Bott, Katie Bouch, Benjamin Boudreaux, Maria Bowen, Nicole Boyar, Tara Bradley, Carolina Braunschweig, Ruby Bremer, Emily

Breunig, Ben Brewer, Thomas Brierly, Sara Bright, Kiara Brinkman, Cindy Brinkman, Eleanor Brockman, Roxanne Brodeur, Leslie Brown, David Brown, Joel Brown, David Brownell, Leora Broydo Vestel, Shannon Bryant, Clarissa Buck, Lauren Bundy, Pamela Burdak, Nicole Burgund, Ben Burke, Lynn Burnett, Patrick Burns, Brenna Burns, Bob Burnside, Mateo Burtch, Amy Burton, Graig Butz, Elizabeth Cabral, Jonathan Callard, Stephanie Campbell, Diane Campese, Paul Caparotta, Carin Capolongo, Sandra Cardoza, Virginia Cardozo, Todd Carnam, Anthony Carrillo, Ian Carruthers, Michael Carson, Peggy Cartwright, Michael Case, Marty Castleberg, Michael Catano, Pamela Caul, Michael Cavanaugh, Ann Marie Cavosora, Halsey Chait, Rachel Chalmers, Christy Chan, Eugenia Chan, Bonnie Chan, Momo Chang, Julie Chanter, Eva Chao, Jake Chapnick, Craig Charnley, Evan Chase, Nelly Chauvel, Ana Chavier, Harold Check, George Chen, Candace Chen, Ie-chen Cheng, Tina Cheng, Marianna Cherry, Sekai Chideya, Eugenia Chien, Annie Chiles, Deborah Chilvers, Paul Chilvers, Michael Ching, Stefanie Chinn, Nancy Chirinos, Alex Chisholm, Felix Chon, Kathy Chong, Mike Chorost, David Chow, Felix Chow, Samuel Christian, Thomas Chupein, Tim Chupein, Nick Cimiluca, Adam Cimino, Cristin Ciner, Kimberly Ciszewski, Madeline Clare, Tanya Clark, Erin Clarke, Kevin Cline, Christopher Cobb, Amy Cohen, Emily Cohen, Kathleen Cohn, August Cole, David Cole, Jillian Collins, Monica Contois, Joe Conway, Claire Conway, Christopher Cook, Martha Cooley, Erin Cornelius, John Cornwell, William Cornwell, Malaika Costello-Dougherty, Mary Ann Cotter, Katherine Covell, Gianmaria Cranchini, Caitlin Craven, Will Craven, Spencer Cronk, Amy Crossin, Gregory Crouch, Kimberly Crszewski, Zan Cukor, Kevin Cummins, Ami Cuneo, Bobby Cupp, Jessica Curiale, Bethany Currin, Roberta D'Alois, Nick D'Onofrio, Colin Dabkowski, John Daigre, Veronia Dakota, Kristen Daniel, Michael Davidson, Elizabeth Davidson, Devin Davis, Misty Dawn-Gaubatz, Meara Day, Ashia De la Bastide, Mark De la Vina, Maria De Lorenzo, Liz Dedrick, Shannon DeJong, James Dekker, Ashia Delabastide, Laura Delizonna, Natisha Demko, Sarah Dennis, Michael DePaul, Marcella Deproto, Kenwyn Derby, Corina Derman, Joey Deschenes, Christine Dibiasi, Pamela Dickson, Nada Djordjerich, Colin Dobrowski, Kathleen Dodge, Katrina Dodson, Nick Donofrio, Gina Donohoe, Carrie Donovan, Amy Donsky, Denise Dooley, John Douglass, Jenny Doyle, Julia Doyle, Norman Doyle, Marie Drennan, Marcie Dresbaugh, Maureen Duffy, Emma Dunbar, Lisa Duran, Miles Durrance, Sidra Durst,

Diane Durst, Leila Easa, Nathaniel Eaton, Issac Ebersole, Jeffrey Edalatpour, Katie Edmonds, Booh Edourado, Tom Edwards, Rob Ehle, Cindy Ehrlich, Alison Ekizian, Eve Ekman, Stephen Elliott, Jeff Elliott, Kristine Ellis, Katherine Emery, Toria Emery, Christina Empedodes, Michelle Eng, Michael Eng, Deborah England, Damien English, Ken Ensslin, Elizabeth Esfahani, Adam Estes, Denise Esteves, Starla Estrada, Ian Evans, Maureen Evans, Ted Everson, Adam Faber, Gabrielle Falzone, Katie Farnsworth, Doug Favero, Deborah Fedorchuk, Daniel Fee, Sam Felsing, Janet Ference, Windy Ferges, Peter Finch, Ian Fink, Anthony Firestine, Jamie Flam, Jennifer Fleisher, Jane Flint, Ryan Foley, Mark Follman, Sarah Fontaine, Chantal Forfota, Tammy Fortin, Katie Fowley, Ilona M. Fox, Lara Fox, Mary Foyder, Laura Fraenza, Jennifer Frances, Gianmaria Francini, Kevin Francis, Chance Fraser, Katie Fraser, Wendy Freedman, Lisa Friedman, Danielle Friedman, Milli Frisbie, Nick Frontino, Danni Fruehe, Laurel Gaddie, Jason Galeon, Tanya Gallardo, Elizabeth Gannes, Theresa Ganz, Kathy Garlick, Derek Garnett, John Garrison, Petrice Gaskin, Heather Gates, Nicholas Gattig, Misty Gaubatz, Linda Gebroe, Joan Gelfand, Bruce Genaro, Chris Gerben, Beth Gerber, Jeremy Gershen, Antonia Giannoccaro, Alex Giardino, John Gibler, Cristina Giner, Dan Gingold, Michael Ginther, Marie Glancy, Debra Glass, Daniel Glendening, Jenny Glennon, Lianna Glodt, Nicole Gluckstern, Robert Glushko, Carrie "Charly" Godwin, Aimee Goggins, Mark Goldberg, Rebecca Goldman, Lis Goldschmidt, Rachel Goldstein, Rebecca Golman, Ellen Goodenow, Anastasia Goodstein, Corinne Goria, Tom Gorman, Mark Gotelli, Allie Gottlieb, Nelson Graff, Vanessa Grahl, Brian Gray, Douglas Gray, Susan Gray, Soru Gray, Rachel Greenberger, Josh Greene, Sarah Grierson, Kyle Griffiths, Scott Grinsell, Pamela Grisman, Lauren Groff, Cristal Guderjahn, Erin Gulbengay, Louis Gurman, Leslie Guttman, Daniel Habib, Jennifer Hahn, Sally Haims, Alanna Hale, Holly Hale, Tika Hall, Wesley Hall, Christopher Hall, Jonah Hall, Lauren Halsted, Leslie Hamanaka, Elissa Hamlat, Hana Hammer, Marie Hamre, Dodie Han, Yosh Han, Jamie Hand, Sandra Handler, Sean Hanratty, Howard Harband, Ellen Harding, Michael Harkin, Leora Harling, Reyhan Harmanci, Elliot Harmon, Ian Hart, Kieran Hartsough, Doug Hawkins, Ingrid Hawkinson, Kristen Hawkinson, Noah Hawley, Heather Hax, Jonathon Hayes, Michael Hays, Carol Hazenfield, Justine Hebron, Micaela Heekin, Lisa Heer, Meredith Heil, Eric Hellweg, Jessica Hemerly, Stacey Hendren, Cheryl Hendrickson, Christine Hendrickson, Nora

Hennessy, Kathleen Hennessy, Pamela Herbert, Angela Hernandez, Lucy Herr, Emma Hewitt, Shane Hildebrandt, Wendy Hill, Elizabeth Hille, Kara Hinman, Bonny Hinners, Lynh Ho, Elizabeth Hodder, Eric Hoffman, Katie Hoffman, Catherine Hollis, Allie Holly-Gottlieb, Pamela Holm, Lisa Hom, Matthew Honan, Eli Horowitz, Adria Hou, Hank Hozgrefe, Kristen Hren, Andro Hsu, Amy Huber, Debbie Huey, Justin Hughes, Leslie Humanaka, Bree Humphries, Annie Hunt, Wyatt Hunter, Elizabeth Hurt, Lori Huskey, Phoebe Hyde, Rusti Icenogel, Angela Ingel, Hannah Ingram, Melissa Ip, Lisa Isaacson, Lucy Ives, Ilene Ivins, June Jackson, Malia Jackson, Abigail Jacobs, Nathania Jacobs, Taylor Jacobson, Maggie Jacobstein, Leslie Jamison, Donald Jans, Gail Jardine, Jessica Jarjoura, Nalani Jay, Lee Jens, Lee Jensen, Arne Johnson, Ellen Johnson, Ruth Johnson, Mary Johnson, Ben Johnson, Annie Johnson, Jamie Johnston, Andy Jones, Gerard Jones, Kevin Jones, Ty Jones, Coco Jones, Carolyn Jones, Samantha Jones, Judith Jordan, Brent Jordheim, Erin Jourdan, Matt Joyce, Jessica Kahn, Elizabeth Kahn, Liz Kahn, Ruby Kalson-Bremer, Arya Kamangar, Joshua Kamler, Garrett Kamps, John Kane, Monica Karaba, Crystal Karabelas, Michelle Karell, Emily Katz, Dan Kaufman, Lynne Kaufman, Veronica Kavass, Aaron Kayce, Lindsay Keach, Tom Kealey, Sean Paul Keating, Sarah Keefe, Elizabeth Keenley, Betsy Keever, E.K. Keith, Matthew Kelley, Maria Kelley, Leslie Kelly, Craig Kelly, Glenn Kelman, Christina Kelso, Elizabeth Kennedy, Evan Kennedy, Michelle Kiefel, Jon Kiefer, Aaron Kierbel, Klover Kim, Tae Kim, Meaghan Kimball, Kristi Kimball, Jennifer King, Martha Kinney, Sasha Kinney, James Kinsman, Deborah Kirk, Ginevra Kirkland, Susanna Kittredge, Shari Kizirian, Suzanne Kleid, Stephanie Klein, Kevin Kline, Metha Klock, Keith Knight, Scott Knippelmeir, Conan Knoll, Linda Knox, Sarah Kobrinsky-Kleinzahler, Rodney Koeneke, Kate Kokontis, Suji Kong, Lee Konstantinou, Gabriel Kram, Jacob Kramer, Susie Kramer, Caroline Kraus, Joel Krauska, Ann Krilanovich, Daniel Kristen, Kate Kudirka, Adrian Kudler, Erin Kuka, Angela Kung, Peter Kupfer, Stephanie Kurteff, Trevor Kuski, Nick Kwaan, Adrienne LaBonte, Nina Lacour, Leslie Ladow, Marisa Lagos, Linda Lagunas, Sarah Lahey, Leslie Lambert, Angie Landau, Julie Landry, Adam Lane, Andrea Laue, Adam Lauridsen, Devorah Lauter, Kathryn Lavin, Jeremey Lavoi, Vi T. Le, Galen Leach, Shelly Leachman, John Lee, Kevin Lee, Lisa Lee, Laura LeeMoorhead, Frances Lefkowitz, Victoria Legg, Rachel Leibrock, Andrew Leland, Jacob Leland, Jenee LeMarque, Peter Lennox-King, Chad Lent, Lynn Lent, Shari Leskowitz, Barajas Leticia, Margarita

Levantovskaya, Shira Levine, Mike Levy, Erica Lewis, Kenya Lewis, Kristina Lewis, Jennifer Lewis, Gayle Leyton, Geoffrey Libby, Chid Liberty, Sarah Lidgus, Elyse Lightman, Marilee Chang Lin, Colby Lind, Natalie Linden, Meagan Linn, Andrew Lipnick, Seth Liss, Candice Liu, Colleen Lloyd, Chrissy Loader, Marco Loeb, Scott Loganbill, Grace Loh, Mimi Pei Yee Lok, Joanne Long, David Looby, Gregory Loome, Jemma Lorenat, Jenny Lovold, Amber Lowi, Kok Lye, Amy Lyman, Alexis Lynch, Rachel Lyon, Dantia MacDonald, Amanda Machi, Anthony Macias, Karen Macklin, Beth Macom, Danika Maddocks, Kristen-Paige Madonia, Monica Maduro, Eric Magnuson, Sarah Malashock, Aimee Male, Mary Ann Malkos, Patricia Maloney, Ryan Mammarella, Maya Manian, Sara Mann, Lisa Manolius, Lisa Manter, Peter Marcus, Scott Marengo, Frank Marquardt, Davi Marra, Jamie Marron, Chelsea Martin, Megan Martin, Jerome Martinez, Margaret Mason (Berry), Jennifer Massoni, Laura Mathers, John Maxey, Julie Mayhew, Brie Mazurek, Jennifer "Lulu" McAllister, PK McBee, Taryn McCabe, Michael McCarrin, Katherine McCarthy, Margaret McCarthy, Laura McClure, Sarah McCoy, Kate McDonough, Ryan McFadden, Faith McGee, Nancy McGee, Doug McGray, Dan McHale, June McKay, Lorien McKenna, Terence McKeown, John "Riley" McLaughlin, Jonathon McLeod, Heather McMurphy, John McMurtrie, Colleen McVearry, Frederick Mead, Sierra Melcher, Sarah Melikian, Tessa Melvin, Molly Meng, Hilary Merril, Hilary Merrill, Tamsen Merrill, Robert Merryman, Ray Mertens, Adam Metz, Julia Meuse, Burton Meyer, Talya Meyers, Matthew Micari, Erika Mielke, Amy Miles, Erin Milgram, Kathleen Miller, Nicole Miller, Salome Milstead, Sonia Minden, Logan Mirto, Therese Mitros, Greta Mittner, Krista Mitzel, Tara Mocsny, Keri Modrall, Tom Molanphy, Robyn Moller, Elizabeth Montalbano, Alia Moore, Annie Marie Moore, Elizabeth Moore, Lou Moore, Natalie Moore, Sara Moore, Irene Moore, Jesse Moore, Laura Moorhead, Irene Moosen, Ana Moraga, Abner Morales, Bozena Mercedes Morawski, Mathew Morgan, Samantha Morgan, Kathleen Morgan, Chana Morgenstern, Dominique Morrison, Jennifer Morton, Gary Moskowitz, Joe Mud, Amelia Mularz, Joohee Muromcew, Pat Murphy, Colin Murphy, Colin Murray, Talia Muscarella, Alan Mutter, Brian Myrtetus, Nish Nadaraja, Jay Nalani, Alysha Naples, Sheila Nazzaro, Christina Needham, Ali Neff, Jennifer Nellis, Katherine Nelson, Christopher Nelson, Amie Nenninger, Emberly Nesbitt, Matt Ness, Nick Neuman, Laurel Newby, Conrad Newman, Michael Nichols,

Krista Niles, Jack Nixon, Nick Noack, Mark Noack, Emilie Noble, Joanna Normoyle, Monica Norton, Martin Nouvell, Ryan Novack, Nina Nowack, Joselyn Nussbaum, Risa Nye, Lori Nygaard, Colleen O'Connor, Aimee O'Donnell, Ryan O'Donnell, Suzanne O'Kelly-Richards, Jen O'Neal, Anna O'Neil, Brigid O'Neil, Ben Ogden, Rebecca Oksner, Kathryn Olney, Nick Olsson, Ilyse Opas, Walt Opie, Edward Opton, Andrea Orr, Karin Elena Orr, Tyler Ortman, Frederick Osborn, Kelly Osmundson, Alisa Ostarello, Emily Ostendorf, Kelly Osterling, Owen Otto, Leslie Outhier, Doris Owyang, Veronica Padilla, Denise Padilla, Jeremy Padow, Adam Paganini, Katie Painter, Sonya Palay, Denny Palmer, Jeni Paltiel, Marco Panella, Alaine Panitch, Jina Park, Julia Parmer, Dilaria Parry, Larissa Parson, Matt Parsons, Jessica Partch, Peretz Partensky, Aljay "Jay" Pascua, Shireen Pasha, Stephanie Pau, Kate Pavao, Solveig Pederson, Wade Peerman, Angelica Perez, Clare Perry, C. Elizabeth Perry, Charlotte Petersen, Sarah Peterson, Mary Petrosky, Heather Pez, Nicki Pfaff, Brian Pfeffer, Kristy Phillips, Craig Phillips, Sue Pierce, Micah Pilkington, Ron Piovesan, Melissa Pocek, Shelby Polakoff, Ben Polansky, Paula Ponsetto, Rebecca Poretsky, Jeff Porter, Daria Portillo, Miriam Posner, Lisa Post, Erin Potts, Todd Pound, Angie Powers, Natalie Powers, Peter Prato, Sara Press, Kelly Pretzer, Andrew Price, Melissa Price, Wandee Pryor, Dina Pugh, Conan Putnam, Jason Qin, Carter Quigg, Therese Quinlan, Harvey Rabbit, Mark Rabine, Julie Racioppo, Naomi Raddatz, Kismet Ragab, Sabrina Ramos, Abby Ramsden, Vanessa Raney, Greg Rasmussen, Kerry Ratza, Jane Rauckhorst, Arena Reed, Amy Rees, Kazz Regelman, Karen Regelman, Dalia Regos, Minnie Reichek, Carolyn Reid, Vanessa Reid, Jennifer Reiley, Jennifer Reimer, Ken Reisman, Samantha Remeika, Cathy Remick, Sarah Rhyins, Sarah Rich, Carol Richards, Christina Richardson, Danielle Richardson, Rachel Richardson, Nicki Richensin, Jessica Richman, Matt Ridella, Jen Rios, Amaya Rivera, Becka Robbins, Jason Roberts, Angela Roberts, Lailah Robertson, Blake Robin, Julia Robinson, Lissa Robinson, Barbara Robinson, Laurie Robinson, James Rocchi, Katherine Rochemont, Erica Roe, Brian W. Rogers, Sage Romano, Sarah Roos, Mischa Rosenberg, Seth Rosenberg, Lily Rosenman, Robert Rosenthal, Seth Rosenthal, Ruth Rosenthal, Monica Ross, Elana Roston, Gabriel Roth, Meika Rouda, Rosey Rouhana, Hilary Rubicam-Merrill, Shari Rubin, Rebbeca Rubin, Paul Rueckhaus, Christina Ruiz-Esparza, Maddy Russell-Shapiro, Chris Ryan, Shannon Ryan, Michelle Ryan, Lisa Ryers, Dana Sacchetti, Sarahjane

Sacchetti, Mary Beth Sacchi, Shirazi Sahar, Nora Salim, Clint Sallee, Azmeer Salleh, Eleanor Sananman, Anthony Sanchez, Victoria Sanchez, Paul Sauer, Denise Sauerteig, Laura Schadler, Mary Schaefer, Eric Schaible, Karen Schaser, Deborah Schatten, Sydney Schaub, Erica Scheidt, Stephanie Schenkel, Dana Schmidt, Heidi Schmidt, Kellie Schmitt, Irit Schneider, Samantha Schoech, Ariana Schoellhorn, Laura Scholes, Charles Schoonover, Kate Schox, Jennifer Schwartz, Ana Schwartzman, Patrick Scott, Tracy Seeley, Elizabeth Shafer, Rebecca Shapiro, Dayna Shaw, Adam Shemper, Eli Sheridan, Vaughn Shields, Sahar Shirazi, Pasha Shireen, Dave Shlachter, Mischa Shoni, Zachary Shore, Joshua Siegel, Sam Silverstein, Catherine Silvestre, Michelle Simotas, Rachel Simpson, Saurabhi Singh, Rosemary Slattery, Liana Small, Gordon Smith, Scott Smith, Kerry Smith, Julia Smith, Brian Smith, Carole Snitzer, John Snyder, Adrienne So, Robert Solley, Gloria Son, Faith Songco, Lavinia Spalding, Eric Spitznagel, Sandra Square, Charlene St. John, Kim-Lan Stadnick, Jayne Lyn Stahl, Sandra Staklis, Miruna Stanica, Clifford Stanley, Brian Stannard, Jill Stauffer, Tabitha Steager, Maya Stein, Zach Steinman, Paul Stelhe, Marla Stener, Jon Stenzler, Joanne Sterbentz, Zack Stern-walker, Marisa Stertz, Maria Steuer, Ian Stewart, Tavia Stewart, Jeanine Stickle, Dusty Stokes, Susanne Stolzenberg, Sarah Stone, Dan Strachota, Susan Stranger, Andrew Strickman, Sandra Stringer, Andrew Strombeck, Cora Stryker, Jeff Stryker, Kim Stuart, Harold Stusnick, Dan Sullivan, Reneé Summerfield, Jon Sung, Danica Suskin, Christy Susman, Sigrid Sutter, Constanza Svidler, Anne Swan, Hiya Swanhoyser, Sasha Swartzman, Cicely Sweed, Melanie Swiercinski, Elizabeth Switaj, Andrew Sywak, Rebecca Szeto, Jay Taber, Ronna Tanenbaum, Sarah Tannehill, Cheryl Taruc, Chris Taylor, Krissy Teegerstrom, Yakira Teitel, Emily Teitsworth, Alex Tenorio, Jennifer Terrill, Arul Thangavel, Lisa Tharpe, Evany Thomas, Penelope Thomas, Jason Thompson, Jennifer Thompson, Alison Thompson, Thomas Thornhill, Jeanine Thorpe, Anthea Tjuanakis, Rob Tocalino, Lauren Toker, Sabrina Tom, Chris Tong, Danny Torres, Erik Totten, Vanita Trachte, Jenny Traig, Johnathan Travis, Carol Treadwell, Cary Troy, Richard Trudeau, Jason Turbow, Andrea Turner, Dan Turner, Dylan Tweney, Zoe Urann, Caitlin Van Dusen, Anjel Van Slyke, Vauhini Vara, Mari Vargo, Victor Vasquez, Chloe Veltman, Andrew Vennari, Dan Verel, Vendela Vida, Alfa Villaflor, Michelle Vizinau-Kvernes, Todd von Ammon, Jessica von Brachel, Rafael Vranizan, Andrew Wagner, Megan Wagstaffe, Kate Wahl, Maria Walcutt, Jeff Walker, Melissa Wang, Jen Wang, Alison Wannamaker,

Keef Ward, Mary Warden, Catharine Wargo, James Warner, John Washington, Malena Watrous, Ethan Watters, Gretchen Weber, Lisa Webster, Laurie Weed, Joshua Wein, Debbie Weinberg, Carol Weinstein, Gabe Weisert, Daniel Weiss, Greta Weiss, Jennifer Wells, Amelie Wen, Jess Wendover, Matt Werner, Misty West, Phoebe Westwood, Christine Whalen, Shannon Wheeler, Jonathan White, Brandt Wicke, Greg Wiercioch, Terrye Wilder, Eric Wilinski, Doug Wilkins, Tom Wilkinson, Tanya Wilkinson, Moira Williams, Apphia Williams, Meghann Williams, Jessica Williams, Sean Williford, Carolyn Wilson-Koerschen, Johnathan Winawer, Charles Wincorn, Cabala Windle, Rebecca Winterer, Stephanie Witherspoon, Valerie Witte, Rick Wolfgram, Andy Wong, Grace Wong, May Woo, Maggie Wooll, Naomi Worthington, Liz Worthy, Chris Wrede, Alexis Wright, Jenny Wu, Sinclair Wu, Wendy Wu, David Wygant, Jon Wynacht, Michelle Yacht, Jim Yagmin, Linda Yankowsky, Miranda Yaver, Kristen Yawitz, Kristina Yee, Matthew Yeoman, Chellis Ying, Chris Ying, Ed Yoon, Barbara Yu, Liane Yukoff, Samson Zadmehran, Ricardo Zahra, Elizabeth Zambelli, Nancy Zastudil, Susie Zavala, Emma Zevin, Andrew Ziaja, Brigitte Zimmerman

826 Valencia Programs Overview

We are so proud of the student work collected in this Quarterly. It is the result of countless hours of hard work by students and teachers alike. We are also endlessly inspired by our hard-working tutors, all of whom make the following programs possible. If you have not yet visited 826 Valencia, or if it has been a while, please do come by to see us—we'll treat you to a good mopping, free of charge.

ONE-ON-ONE TUTORING

Five days a week, 826 Valencia is packed with students who come in for free, one-on-one, drop-in tutoring. Some students need help with homework. Others come in to work on ambitious extracurricular projects such as novels and plays. We're particularly proud of our thriving services and support for young students learning English.

WORKSHOPS

826 Valencia also offers free workshops that provide in-depth instruction in a variety of areas that schools don't often include in their curriculum. We've had workshops on writing college-entrance essays and on writing comic books, on preparing for the SAT, on learning software programs, and on producing films. All of the workshops are taught by working professionals and are limited in size, so students get plenty of individual attention. All workshops are project-based and culminate in some sort of product, including plays, chapbooks, videos, and submissions to this Quarterly.

FIELD TRIPS

Three or four times a week, 826 Valencia welcomes an entire class for a morning of high-energy learning. Classes can request a custom-designed curriculum on a subject they've been studying, such as playwriting, or choose from one of our five field trip plans. The most popular is the Storytelling & Bookmaking field trip. In two hours, the students write, illustrate, publish, and bind their own books. They leave with keepsake books and a newfound excitement for writing. Other field trips allow students to meet a local author, to learn the basics of journalism, or to work on a student publication.

IN-SCHOOLS PROGRAM

826 Valencia coordinates an in-schools program that sends tutors directly into classrooms throughout San Francisco. In our biggest in-school project this year, juniors and seniors at Galileo Academy of Science and Technology produced a book of short stories based on each student's family myths and legends. The final product *"Home Wasn't Built In A Day"* included a foreword written by Robin Williams. Throughout the year, 826 Valencia's tutors were found at Everett Middle School helping seventh graders create a guidebook for travelers in the Sahara Desert, working with third-graders at Bryant Elementary who wrote stories about dragons and vampires, and at Leadership High School encouraging seniors through the process of composing their own emotionally-charged speeches based on Hamlet's famous soliloquy. At the Children's Day School, students wrote short stories based on photographs they took in the Mission district with the help of 826 Valencia tutors and volunteers. In the fall, tutors guided students toward com-

pelling essays for their college applications at Galileo High School, Wallenberg High School, John O'Connell High School, and Mission High School. Other programs took place at Buena Vista Elementary School, John Swett Elementary, Horace Mann Middle School, Thurgood Marshall Middle School, and Balboa High School.

826 Valencia runs one full-time in-school project at Everett Middle School: a classroom that has been turned into a pirate-themed Writers' Room. The room is staffed throughout the school year by 826 tutors and volunteers who help students at Everett work on researching, writing, and perfecting their writing assignments. The Everett Writers' Room is also home to the *Straight-Up News*, the school's student newspaper published and edited in collaboration with 826 Valencia. In its third year, the Everett Writers' Room is so successful that every single student at Everett receives one-on-one attention there throughout the school year.

STUDENT PUBLICATIONS

826 Valencia produces a variety of publications, each of which contains work done by students in our various programs. Some students collaborate with professional publishers when their work is chosen for publication, and other students do the majority of the work themselves, writing and producing chapbooks that can be taken home that day. These projects represent some of the most exciting work at 826 Valencia, as they expose and enable Bay Area students to experience a world of publishing otherwise not available to them. Students of 826 Valencia wrote for the following publications:

I Might Get Somewhere: Oral Histories of Immigration and Migration exhibits an array of student-recorded oral narratives about moving to San Francisco from other states in the U.S. and from all over the world. Acclaimed author Amy Tan wrote the foreword to this compelling collection of personal stories, all of which shed light on the problems and pleasures of finding one's life in new surroundings.

Waiting to be Heard: Youth Speak Out about Inheriting a Violent World—thirty-nine students from San Francisco's Thurgood Marshall Academic High School write about the themes of violence and peace, through perspectives that are personal, local, and global. With a foreword by Isabel Allende, the book combines essays, fiction, poetry, and experimental writing pieces to create a passionate collection of student voices.

Talking Back: What Students Know about Teaching is a completely student-produced 140-page paperback book which, in the words of the students, "delivers the voices of the class of 2004 from Leadership High School. In reading this book, currently being used as a required reading textbook at San Francisco State University and Mills College, you will understand the relationships students want with their teachers, how students view classroom life, and how the world affects students."

826 Valencia also publishes scores of chapbooks each semester. These are collections of writing from our workshops, in-school projects, and class projects from schools that team up with us. This year, our most popular titles are: *A Russian Boy in Love, A Horse in Paris, Blue Like Rain, Three Friends Who Were Afraid of the Sun,* and *The Dragon and the Elephant Meet the Pirate.*

The *826 Quarterly* (Volume 6 of which is in your hands at this moment) is put out at least twice a year with writing submitted by youth from all over the San Francisco Bay Area. To submit a story, a poem, a play, or any form of writing you feel would be suitable for publication, please write to quarterly@826valencia.com with your piece attached. Please be sure to include your full name, age, school, and any other pertinent information.

PUBLICATIONS FOR STUDENTS & TEACHERS

Don't Forget to Write, contains fifty-four of the best lesson plans used in workshops taught at 826 Valencia, 826NYC, and 826LA, giving away all of our secrets for making writing fun. Each lesson plan is written by its original workshop teacher, including Jonathan Ames, Aimee Bender, Dave Eggers, Erika Lopez, Julie Orringer, Jon Scieszka, Sarah Vowell, and many more. If you are a parent or teacher, this book is meant to make your life easier, containing enthralling and effective ideas to get your students writing. It was also written as a resource for the aspiring writer; it'll help you with everything from telling your pet a riveting tale, and persuading your parents to your point of view to writing a compelling college essay, and understanding the essay revision process.

826 National

826 Valencia's success is spreading across the country. Under the umbrella of 826 National, tutoring centers are being opened in several cities. If you would like to find out more about other 826 programs, please visit the following websites.

826NYC, www.826nyc.org
826LA, www.826la.org
826 Michigan, www.826michigan.org
826 Chicago, www.826chi.org
826 Seattle, www.826seattle.org

826 National Advisory Board

Erin Bennett

Barb Bersche

Jennifer Bunshoft, Esq.

Nínive Calegari

Dave Eggers

Christopher Frizzelle

Ira Glass

Leah Guenther

Teri Hein

Reece Hirsch

Jay Jacobs

Keith Knight

Tynnetta McIntosh

Bita Nazarian

Alexandra Quinn

Davy Rothbart

Scott Seeley

Steve Seidel

Sarah Vowell

Sally Willcox

I. WORKSHOPS

When the evening rolls in to 826 Valencia, and the pencils are returned to their buckets, we often wonder: Is the writing lab tired? Nearly every day the lab is awakened by the clamor of students visiting for a Storytelling & Bookmaking field trip. This party is followed by a whirlwind drop-in tutoring session where students tackle their homework. But when the sun finally sets, the day is far from over for our steadfast writing lab.

Now the workshop students arrive, armed with their notebooks, and soon the lab is bustling once again. Under its rafters students, ages 6-18, learn to write creatively, efficiently, and confidently through small-group seminars. These workshops address many different exercises in writing—playwriting, short story telling, poetry, comic book writing, investigative journalism—and all are taught by professionals in their field, at no cost to the students.

What follows is a sampling of the outstanding achievements from the last workshop season in our lab. Regretfully, we cannot include every piece fashioned here. If you are young, please come join us. Create your own comic book, explore varied narrative voices, solve a mystery, shape a poem. Write with us!

[*In a collaboration that's become a tradition, two freshman classes from MetWest joined us for six Fridays in a row at the beginning of the 2005–06 school year to write, edit, and publish a collection of short stories. This year, the stories were based on life experiences.*]

Change the Past to Change the Future

by AKEYA HARRIS

Age 15, MetWest High School

"**I**'m glad to have you back with me, sweetie," Mommy says while giving me a kiss on the forehead.

"Well, I'm glad to be back, Mom."

"Baby, tell Mommy about yourself. I haven't seen you in four years and when I did you were only eight."

"Well, let's just say… that I'm out of the pit of hell. I remember when it used to be so hot, even on rainy days. The only way we could cool off was when we went to the river, but even the river was hot. I didn't like it there. Not to mention I had to be with Jude, and I can't tell you how much I hated her. I was jealous and full of envy for her because she took the one thing that mattered to me in this stupid world, and that was you. Mom, remember? We used to go together like peas and carrots, Steve and Blue, Patrick and SpongeBob. You have to admit, I was nothing without you. Then you got pregnant with Jude and forgot all about me. You used to neglect me when it was time for my bedtime stories. I never expressed how I felt, and to be honest, I didn't really know what type of emotion I was feeling, but it really hurt."

"Oh, baby. Mommy is so sorry," she says. She attempts to hug me, but I move away.

"No, don't be. I don't care anymore, but sometimes I wish I could go back in time and fix things that I did wrong, like Jude being born. It's funny. I always wonder how it would be if you guys didn't have Jude, but here's the funny part. I can't ever imagine it. Then I begin to think maybe it was destiny or maybe it was just made to be that way. Then when I look out the window and at the busy streets of Oakland and see the little girls playing double dutch, laughing and giggling, I wish my life could be that way. That's when I wish that my sister and I had had that relationship from the start. But I took the hard road instead. I hated her until it became a habit, an addiction so hard for me to break. I never looked at this situation as 'Jude is the only sibling that I have, and if something were to happen to Mom and Dad, we would have to look out for each other.' I looked at it as, 'You took what was mine and I'll take your life.'"

"Baby, why did you think this way?"

"I don't know why. I just did. Now I'm too old to go back and change things. I know that, but that is why I'm trying to make it better. Anyway, as I was saying, the world revolved around me for a very long time, six years to be exact. Then, when Jude was born, the world switched sides, and that's when the hatred kicked in. That's when I started to wonder about Jude, wonder about what was going on in her life and if it was as bad as I thought mine was. Not that I cared. I just wondered. Come to find out her life was worse than mine.

"In 1999, we moved to Africa and we lived in Accra, the main city of Ghana. It's just like America, with a lot of black folks, and we were used to that since we were from Texas, Tyler to be exact, and it was full of them. Anyway, the only difference was that the women carried food on their heads. I remember the first time I tried to do that it was really hard to balance, but I got it. Do you remember, Mom?"

"Yes, I do. It was amazing to me," she says, thinking of the time we went and how she felt so special.

"Okay, whatever, don't get all sentimental on me. It was so crazy how people ran up to the taxi like we were gods. That kind of scared me but since some of the boys were big and sexy I wasn't worried."

"What did you know about sexy at eight years old?" my mom asks in a joking voice.

"Well, at that time, I didn't know anything about it at all, but when I look back on it, dang, they were fine. Some of them were tall, some medium height, with big muscles and dark, smooth, sexy backs. Wahoo! I'm getting hot all over again."

My mom and I take a moment to laugh.

"We thought that that would be the best place to live. It was exotic and cheap. Yet we, or should I say you, didn't bring enough money, so that's when you had to come back and leave me and Jude with *Dad*. Dad wasn't the best father. He was always drunk and would hit me a lot. That's why it killed me to have to stay with him for four years. It was really hard without you, Mom. We had a lot of experiences I don't think you know about, like the time when we were homeless for two weeks. I mean, we weren't completely homeless like living in a box or something."

"Oh, I thought you were completely homeless," my mom says with a sigh of relief.

"We just were threatened by the landlord all the time and we had to move from hotel to hotel. During this time, I was looking in phone books to try to find some place for us to stay that was cheap and affordable. It's so scary knowing your family's life is in your hands. Soon it came to the point where just as long as there was a roof over our heads, we could bear it whether it was nice or a basement. God blessed me, and I found these African-Americans who gave discounts for newcomers every two months, but we stayed for four. Then we moved to Akwamufie, a small village in Ghana, and that's when the adventure really began. That's when you got mad at Dad and stopped sending money because he spent it on the wrong stuff instead of food. So I had to go sell stuff on my head like the other African girls. I really got caught up in the culture. I cut off my hair, started speaking the language, and started to be just like an average African girl. No, I don't mean I walked naked, but I took care of my heavy burdens, like the feelings that I had about having to take care of my family without you, that's all. Dad started to build the house there after you guys made up and you started to send money again. We moved into the house before it was done. All it had was a half-finished floor, roof, windows, and ceiling, but it was pleasant to know we didn't have to pay bills. Plus it was by this river in the woods called the Akosombo river.

"It was a Sunday, and I was about to cook the Sunday dinner as always. I had told Jude to bring me the chicken to kill. She mumbled under her breath and said she was scared. When I finally got her to bring the stupid chicken, she went somewhere and I didn't really care. I dug my hole in the ground and I tied the chicken's wings behind his back like he was under arrest. I plucked the feathers on his neck so I could make a clean slit. I sharpened the knife on a rock beside me and then I slit the chicken's throat. Then all of a sudden, Jude crept up behind me and said, 'Mmm-mmm-mmm… you have a way of killing things,' in a disappointing tone."

"'What's that supposed to mean?' I asked with curiosity.

"'I mean you destroy everything,' Jude said with a body movement that was like, *I should know.*

"'*Shut up*, before I destroy you,' I said with a flinch at her.

"'Too late, because you already have.'

"Then Jude walked away with limp, sad body language. For some reason, I had tears in my eyes. I wiped them really hard and puckered up as if I was Muhammad Ali's daughter and had just gotten knocked out and then gotten up like it wasn't a problem, but then something calmed me down. I was wondering why Jude would say that. Why would she keep it inside if I was hurting her? Then it occurred to me that that was my whole plan from the day she was born. I felt really bad, but everybody and their mama knew I was too prideful to say I was sorry, especially after all these years. That night at dinner I watched my sister really carefully. She didn't look four at all. She had bags under her eyes and you could tell that she had been crying."

"She looks just like you when you were her age," my mom says, remembering.

"Anyway, after dinner she went into the living room by herself and after I washed the dishes, I went in to purposely bother her, but when I walked in she had the saddest face. Her face said, 'please don't, Mary Lee. You've done enough.'

"So I just said, 'Hey,' acting like nothing had happened.

"'What do you want,' Jude said quietly.

"'See, I was trying to be nice.'

"'No, you were trying to start something,' Jude said.

"'Was not.'

"I knew I was being immature, Mom.

"'Hey, you wanna know what your problem is?' Jude said. 'You just won't let things go.'

"'What are you talking about?'

"'You're just mad because I took your precious mommy,' said Jude in a teasing, provoking voice as she circled me.

"After that it was all over. I felt like I had lost my mind. I grabbed for her neck, and she wiggled her skinny self out and bit my tummy since that was the only place she could reach. I wanted to kill her like I had mercilessly killed that chicken, but my dad split us apart.

"After our fight we were not speaking. When it was time to get ready for school, I poured water on her, and when it was time for dinner, I silently put her food at the table where she normally sat. This was bound to change when Dad was at his sickest. I remember coming into the bedroom. It smelled like must and like alcohol had been seeping through his skin. He was just lying there. As I saw my father struggling for breath, like a fish who had jumped out of the water, I knew it was time to step up, but I was too stubborn. I didn't want to talk to Jude, but then I didn't want my father to die. As I watched his chest go down lower and lower after each gasp, I couldn't take it any more. 'Jude, *quick!* Call the 511 and get me water. *And step on it!*' The 511 was like 911, only they came a lot slower, but as fast as they could, and since we lived in the woods, that was thirty minutes later. My father was still alive, but in the worst condition ever. He looked as pale as a ghost when he held my hand and said, 'Everything will be alright.' He felt like cold wood and his smile looked like skeleton bones.

"I left Jude with one of the villagers who was really sweet and reliable while I checked Daddy into the hospital. The doctor said all that he could do was give Dad a shot, but the rest was up to God. This really scared me and I went home terrified and stressed. When I got back to the village, I picked up Jude and took her home. I fed her and put her to bed. She told me she was too scared to sleep by herself, so I let her sleep with me. For the first time in my life, I held her close to me and I kissed her on the forehead to let her know she was safe. I felt like it was easier to love her than to hate her, and she was not so bad after all. I noticed all the positive things about my sister in those two weeks. She can sing and dance and is an excellent artist.

"When Dad got home, we tried not to fight or argue because he didn't need any more stress. Now here we are, the best of friends. We're both older and we realize we need to take good care of each other because when you and Dad are long gone, we will need each other. I'm working on being a better sister to Jude. I don't want her past to form her future, and I'm doing all I can to fix things, like reading her bedtime stories and taking her to the park. When I don't feel like talking, I don't yell at her. I just tell her, 'Mary Lee is not here at the moment so could you please leave a message after the beep?' She really leaves a message and I really get back to her. I'm getting better at it, Mom, little by little, day by day."

As my mom looks at the family picture on the wall, with me and Jude under a tree, our heads together, hugging each other, she says, "Yes you are, baby, yes you are."

[*This workshop explored the powers of the narrator through individual writing and group improvisation exercises. First the students took a look at a few famous narrators to see how those narrators tell their stories. The students then entered the scene of a crime, discovering that what actually happens takes on a life of its own with each witness's account.*]

The Case of the Sparkly Pink Hello Kitty Pen

by EMILY MAYER
Age 13, Lick-Wilmerding High School

Part 1: Margo

She told me it was her sparkly pink Hello Kitty pen. I disagreed. It was always hers, never mine, and her excuses that my property was rightfully hers had, over the past few months, grown a tad unbelievable. Sheryl had been my steadfast best friend from the moment we lay eyes on each other in Mrs. Loden's kindergarten classroom with the rainbow posters and all the dolls in the world for us to invent stories for. I was fascinated by her plastic heart-shaped sunglasses that gave you a twin when you looked at them from the front, while she was entranced by my purple Barbie shoelaces I just got for my "fourth and a half" birthday. That was the first trade of our friendship. And now, they had gone way too far. You know that girl you hate to love? That was Sheryl to me. She always had to be in control. The princess. I, the carriage conductor. But now, I was going to stand up to her. "You can't have it," I told her, my arms folded tightly across my chest. But sometimes people just won't give up. I was about to use my weak arms to pull it from her when Tommy, her baby brother, waddled in. And I, making sure it wasn't her mom or dad, or someone who would catch my act of shame, thrust my hand into her pocket. The pen fell on the floor. And as in slow motion, Tommy grabbed it in his little tattle-tale fist and chewed it. Sheryl and I both instinctively made faces of disgust and walked out, in order to paint our nails with the Hello Kitty plastic pink polish that came with the pen.

Part 2: Sheryl

How could she possibly say no? Had she ever said no before? Had the letters "n" and "o" together ever left her lips and reached my ear before now? I don't think so. I have always been in control. She's always done what I've told her to do, no questions asked. It's not fair! The pink Hello Kitty pen called my name, spoke to me, I swear. And so I took it. Isn't that how it has always been? I just knew she wasn't using the pen the right way. It's such a pretty pen. So sparkly and pink. So I took it. At least I could use it and appreciate it right. But then she, my very best friend in the whole wide world, betrayed me, sticking her dirt-caked hands into my new jasmine princess jacket. She stole it and it's not fair. But at least she didn't get to touch it for too long. Tommy, my gross, cootie-catching baby brother, trundled in and, using his slimy grip, stuck it into his mouth and chewed on it. The marker was lost to the cootie king forever. I almost gasped with horror. I looked at Margo, and she looked at me. And I remembered her brand-new nail polish and smiled. And she, I guess, realized her wrong and smiled back. With one last glance of disgust, we flounced our hair and turned away. Here we were, Sheryl the princess and her faithful servant Margo, making a comeback.

[*This workshop explored the powers of the narrator through individual writing and group improvisation exercises. First the students took a look at a few famous narrators to see how those narrators tell their stories. The students then entered the scene of a crime, discovering that what actually happens takes on a life of its own with each witness's account.*]

Flowers in Her Hair

by EMILY MAYER

Age 13, Lick-Wilmerding High School

How refreshing it was for her to be outside with fresh, cool, saltwater air blowing through her hair and into her ears and eyes and nose. The dank smell of decaying flesh and widows mourning had haunted her for months, invading every private moment and single breath. And now she was emancipated from the darkness of death. Living life, being alive, felt as it never had before. She had been numb, walking through life like a ghost, seeing everything and yet nothing at all. Even the cold air, the threatening air ripping against her raw skin, felt joyous. And yet, it was a quiet sort of joy, a second in which she realized she was happy, one thought without tragedy. And the sunny flowers her two younger siblings had shyly handed to her prickled against her coarse black hair, providing stunning contrast to her life before and after the war.

The freshly starched collar of the shirt made her neck itch intensely, and the childish air that emanated from it disagreed with her heart and gut. She resisted the puffed sleeves and tight waist of her pinafore, wishing more than anything to feel her skin against the worn peasant clothes that had brought her family together in their race for survival. That was what they had gained: the trust, the honesty. And now she was back in front of the upright eyes of the camera, her family's silent inverted face surrounding her on all sides.

[*Poet-Free: Free the Poet in You!* was an introduction to poetry taught by Michelle Ryan in the Fall of 2005. Students learned about language, rhyme, metaphor, and other poetic tools. They also had the opportunity to free-write and share the results aloud with their classmates.]

Robby's Poem

by ROBBY STOSICK
Age 10, Lafayette Elementary

My teacher's rats hate to shave pencils.
Zippy ate the computer lab. Peanut ate a seventy-ton Zippy.
The computer bit its way out of Peanut's stomach.
Then the computer ate the school and Zippy.
The camera's flash lit up the world.
The talking atlas consumed the continents.
My dog drank all the water and ate the universe.
The mechanical pencils ran out of ideas.
Does 826 Valencia eat movies?
A dog ate you!

HOW TO BORE EVERYONE TO DEATH

[This workshop was a study in academic essay writing that was not boring in itself and, because of insurance concerns, there was no actual "death" involved. Students experimented with the new (and often misunderstood) cutting-edge writing technology known as "boringness theory," to learn what boring writing is. We feel this is a perfect example of boring writing.]

About Mariah Carey

by BRENDAN SASSO
Age 17, Terra Nova High School

My speech is about Mariah Carey. She was born on August 3, 1972. Her favorite color is pink. Her favorite insect is the Monarch butterfly. She was homecoming queen in her high school. Her senior quote was, "Be true to yourself." She met the head of Columbia records at a party. She gave him her demo tape. Now she's famous. She has a dog named Fluffy.

HOW TO BORE EVERYONE TO DEATH

[This workshop was a study in academic essay writing that was not boring in itself and, because of insurance concerns, there was no actual "death" involved. Students experimented with the new (and often misunderstood) cutting-edge writing technology known as "boringness theory," to learn what boring writing is. Here's another example of boring writing.]

Boring Paragraph

by CLAIRE WILLIAMS
Age 16, Drew School

I pulled into the parking lot around 1:30 in the afternoon. There was nowhere to park. I pulled out and drove around the corner—no parking on the street, either. I turned back around and checked in the parking lot again. There was a spot. I pulled in, but the car was crooked. I put the car in reverse, backed up, and turned my wheels. I pulled back into the spot. I turned the car off and got out. I walked through the front door of the store. Sal waved. I said, "Hello."

HOW TO BORE EVERYONE TO DEATH

[This workshop was a study in academic essay writing that was not boring in itself and, because of insurance concerns, there was no actual "death" involved. Students experiment-ed with the new (and often misunderstood) cutting-edge writing technology known as "bor-ingness theory," to learn what boring writing is. Conversely, students practised composing non-boring pieces. Below is an example.]

The Throbbing Arm
and the Spinning Ballroom

by PHOEBE MORGAN *&* SIOBHAN WILLING

Ages 14 & 15, Drew School & home schooled

Phoebe Morgan's inner elbow is in extensive pain. It is in heart-staking, excruciating, throbbing pain. It's the kind of pain that one would need a cement truck full of morphine to get rid of. Phoebe Morgan doesn't believe she has ever experi-enced such massive pain in her life. She doesn't know how anyone could tolerate it. She thinks that she will go on a chainsaw killing rampage induced by this terrible misfortune.

The actual injury consists of a gruesome, scarring gash on top of a pulsating, deep, mauveish-green bruise—a true beauty mark of death. Although Phoebe cannot comprehend that this horrid pain could get worse, if she doesn't take care of it, it may become infect-ed. She doesn't want to aid it in its healing, for fear of the alcoholic sting of the solution known as hydrogen peroxide (which, by the way, is *disgusting* to gargle).

The ghastly injury was the result of the following incident. The howling twilight wind had the same miserable moan as that of an innocent child being tortured by a homicidal maniac. The air in the ballroom (a ballroom that had once been grand and glamorous, but was now dusty and decrepit) was cool, as eager fingers had previously pried open the windows.

The cumbersome mistress Siobhan Willing came deliriously stumbling in, champagne glass in hand, heading for Phoebe, the delicate damsel cowering in the far corner of the cobweb-infested chamber.

"Dance with me, darling," Siobhan blubbered, alcohol leaking from the sides of her mouth, as she snatched Phoebe's quivering wrist from her fragile chest.

"Never, you wretched hag!" Phoebe exclaimed, haughtily tossing back her violet locks. With this remark, Siobhan bared her teeth in an animalistic sneer and proceeded to wrap her sweaty, skeletal hands around Phoebe's pale, swan-like neck, causing her body to crumble limply to the marble floor, and forcing her naïve mind into demonic fantasies involving dairy products.

When the fragile Ms. Morgan awoke, it was to discover a perfectly Y–shaped incision carved into her virginal, lily-white inner elbow, by the switchblade of God himself. "What does it mean?!" whispered the Mistress Willing, now sobered by shock at her own actions.

"God wants to know why you do it, Siobhan, God wants to know!" Phoebe cried from her rose-bud lips.

Siobhan sobbed in her hand, then howled to the enraged, thunder-striking heavens. "I'll never do it again! Never, ever, EVER!" And with this she proceeded to dash into the kitchen wing and to flush every drop of liquid down the tub-like, jewel-encrusted sink.

And thus, the Y–shaped scar remains, a reminder of the night that changed their lives… FOREVER!

[*In this workshop for students 8–11, the authors got to plan an imaginary dinner party, deciding what exciting guest would be coming to dinner, planning the menus, writing fanciful invitations, and outlining the entertainment that would accompany the meal. No imaginary expense was spared to assure the special guests a memorable evening.*]

My Great Dinner Party

by CORINNA TAM

Age 7, Alamo Elementary School

One day I called Emily. We talked about having a dinner party at the mall that I built. Then we wrote the invitations.

Everybody came at 2:00 PM! We ate, slept, played games, and did lots more. Then we had a pillow fight.

[*In this workshop for students 8–11, the authors got to plan an imaginary dinner party, deciding what exciting guest would be coming to dinner, planning the menus, writing fanciful invitations, and outlining the entertainment that would accompany the meal. No imaginary expense was spared to assure the special guests a memorable evening.*]

My Great Dinner Party
Caution: Rated "R"

by ELLIOT TAM

Age 9, Alamo Elementary School

"Hooray! It's Halloween!" Everybody ran to the newest place in town, Vampire's Bloody Graduation. I invited them and it was my treat.

If you were at the party you would have seen: Yoda, Mew Two, and Pikachu. You could also have seen Link, Kirby, and Bugs Bunny entertaining. After everybody was there we ate dinner. We had blood, blood, humans, and more blood.

After dinner we had dessert. For dessert we had money. Some people were full so they just kept the $3,941,567,208. At the end of the party, we sang "Good Riddance" and walked home.

[This story was written in Jacqueline Moses's Wallenberg High class in a 4-session workshop taught by Dave Eggers. The students were given Jamaica Kincaid's short story "Girl," wherein a girl receives a seemingly endless, sometimes contradictory list of instructions from her mother, and the students were asked—in twenty minutes—to write similar pieces, illustrating the instructions, obligations and pressures they personally live with.]

Good Cajun Daughter

by ROZ LABEAN
Age 17, Wallenberg High School

Don't wash the dishes like that because you use too much water. Why can't you cook like your mother? Why can't you look like your sister? Why aren't you as good an actress as her? You have to get good grades. You have to go to college. Why can't you just lose weight so that boys will like you? If you don't shape up you will be a disgrace to the Richard name. What happened to the normal daughter I raised? Why can't you clean regularly? I've told you a thousand times how to fry that catfish and you mess it up every darn time. You won't marry because you aren't a good Cajun daughter. Once you can cook, clean, and raise the kids, I'll respect you. Until then you don't deserve my respect.

[*This story was written in Jacqueline Moses's Wallenberg High class in a 4-session workshop taught by Dave Eggers. The students were given Jamaica Kincaid's short story "Girl," wherein a girl receives a seemingly endless, sometimes contradictory list of instructions from her mother, and the students were asked—in twenty minutes—to write similar pieces, illustrating the instructions, obligations and pressures they personally live with.*]

Girl Story

by ESHER JONES ESTEVES
Age 16, Wallenberg High School

Be home at 4:30. Do all your homework and chores. Stop wearing shorts and miniskirts because the guys in the streets might say something to you and I'm sure you wouldn't like it. Don't give your number to any boys except the guys that I know. Tell them you can't have a boyfriend until you're eighteen so that they'll stop hollerin'. If someone is trying to fight you, let them hit you first and then you do the rest. Always keep your head up. Don't let anyone put you down. Turn your phone on every time you have it. We will be calling you every hour to make sure you're okay.

WRITING WORKSHOP

[*Dave Eggers conducted a 4-session workshop with students at Wallenberg High School. For this in-class exercise, students were asked to adopt an unfamiliar persona, and write a letter from that person/animal/thing. All the letters were mailed; confusion ensued.*]

Book's Letter

by PEERAPAT TEERAWATTANASOOK

Age 18, Wallenberg High School

Hello. I have always seen you in room 211, in the morning when your students slowly pass me and my friends out. We just sit on their desks until you tell them what page to open to. I hate it when you don't give them the page number and only tell them, "Open the book to where we left off yesterday." Oh man I hate that!! They go through all my pages, back and front, for a long time, until they finally find the right page.

You're the teacher, right? Well I am too. We both have the same job, to teach kids. But why can't I move around like you? You move around so fast compared to the students. You always walk around full of charged energy, while the students are slow. I wish I could move around like you. I'm jealous; it's bad enough that I can't move, then you stack my friends on top of me.

Please stop stacking me, and also start telling them the page to open to from now on. I'm tired of being flipped around. If possible, tell your students to handle me and my friends more carefully. That way you wouldn't have to find books to replace me.

I heard they burn "old" books, is that true? PLEASE DON'T FIND

OTHER BOOKS TO REPLACE ME. Thank you for your time. Please remember not to replace me...

Signed,
Your Yellow Book

WRITING WORKSHOP

[*This story was written in Jacqueline Moses's Wallenberg High class in a 4-session workshop taught by Dave Eggers. The students were given Jamaica Kincaid's short story "Girl," wherein a girl receives a seemingly endless, sometimes contradictory list of instructions from her mother, and the students were asked—in twenty minutes—to write similar pieces, illustrating the instructions, obligations and pressures they personally live with.*]

The Daily Phone Call from Mom

by VICKY GUAN

Age 17, Wallenberg High School

Did you do your homework yet?
Yeah. I'm doing it right now.
Did you do your laundry yesterday?
No, it's not full yet.
Were you late to school yesterday?
No. Just ten minutes.
What did you eat for lunch today?
I forgot.
Did you take a shower yet?
No. Later.
Shower now so you won't be in the way of other
    people.
Okay.
Did you have breakfast today?
No. I didn't have time.
Why are you always late to school? How many times
    have I told you to not be late?
Um...

Do you even want to go to school?
Yes, Mom… I—
What did you eat for dinner?
Do your homework.
I am!
Remember to do your laundry.
Don't go out today.
Take care of your baby cousin.
What are you doing?
Sigh… Nothing…
I gotta go back to work now.
Bye.

WRITING WORKSHOP

[*This story was written in Jacqueline Moses's Wallenberg High class in a 4-session workshop taught by Dave Eggers. The students were given Jamaica Kincaid's short story "Girl," wherein a girl receives a seemingly endless, sometimes contradictory list of instructions from her mother, and the students were asked—in twenty minutes—to write similar pieces, illustrating the instructions, obligations and pressures they personally live with.*]

Think About What You Do

by PHILIP NGUY

Age 16, Wallenberg High School

D o your homework. Change your clothes. Pull up your pants if you don't want to get mobbed by a gang. Never talk back to me. Do you want me to beat you to death? Don't make me kill you. You know if you hadn't done that, I wouldn't have to ground you. Someday you are going to suffer when I die. You could never survive without me. I am not a bad influence on you. The people you hang around are a bad influence on you. You can never go to a college better than the one I went to. I can never trust you. Take out the garbage. Do your chores. If you ever come home late, you will not get your allowance. Don't come in smelling like crap. Take off your hat in the house. I'll burn your clothes if you keep wearing them like that. Take better care of your sister. Stop watching TV. Get off the computer. You have been on it 24/7. Go to sleep earlier. Don't get kicked out of school. If you don't graduate from high school, you'll have to join the army. You are going to be a bum if you don't study hard enough. You can never afford a house. You can never get another chance.

[In this introduction-to-poetry workshop, students, ages 12–16, learned to tap their most powerful memories in order to render abstract concepts concretely. As they became more attuned to the wonders of the everyday, poetry arrived in search of them.]

Fire

by DEVON KEARNEY
Age 14, Basis Charter School

As I dance around in my orange glow,
A strong heat flows from me,
Warming whoever is brave enough to sit at my side.
I can dance for hours.
Many people just stare,
Many people smile,
Others try to take a picture; I never stand still long
    enough for them to focus.
I am light in dark, a place for many to gather.
They come for the light, and stay with me.
I warm anyone who is brave enough to sit at my side.
I can dance for hours, or until I am doused.

[In this introduction-to-poetry workshop, students, ages 12–16, learned to tap their most powerful memories in order to render abstract concepts concretely. As they became more attuned to the wonders of the everyday, poetry arrived in search of them.]

Dragon's Charm

by DEVON KEARNEY

Age 14, Basis Charter School

On wings of thunder, honor bound,
Search me out, I drum the sound.
Twist and turn, in the night
Dragon come, my guiding light.
Protector, guardian, friend not foe
Come to me, see my signal glow.
Strong and true, this friendship charm,
I beckon thee, shield me from harm.
Around and about my magic swirls
Come to me, your wings unfurled.

[In this introduction-to-poetry workshop, students, ages 12–16, learned to tap their most powerful memories in order to render abstract concepts concretely. As they became more attuned to the wonders of the everyday, poetry arrived in search of them.]

Flying Through the Pieces of My Heart

by DEVON KEARNEY

Age 14, Basis Charter School

Laughs, cries, sings
Flying through the pieces of my heart,
A broken pane of glass, shattered in the frame,
Red as blood, dripping with the love I felt.
Now scoop up the broken window, put it back into the fire,
Start anew,
Forge another,
It takes time.
The new window put up, the rain pounding against it,
Stronger than before, still flexing with the wind.
Beat the rain and the fierce wind back.
The storm is over,
Open the window once more,
Let the birds in.
Stronger than before,
It will not break as easily.

[*In this workshop, students, ages 10–12, learned the secrets of great reporters by solving a mystery. The gummy bear trees have been dying and the tangerine forest is a mess. Why? Students interviewed the local tribes, government authorities, shady business owners, and the famous actors who were trying to save the forest. They then used the gathered information to write stories that are rich, vibrant, detail-filled, and interesting to read.*]

Ranger Ranger
Turns into a Bad Tangerine

by EMMA HYNDMAN

Age 10, Clarendon Japanese Bilingual Bicultural Program

D own about four miles off the dirt road is a beautiful tangerine forest. There's no longer a citrusy smell coming from the forest, but a foul, ugly poisonous odor.

Ranger Ranger, the ranger of the forest, said it all started about two months ago; coincidentally, the time he got his obnoxious hiccups. He feels very strongly about his animal friends and is worried about their disappearance.

He told us to speak to Pete Peterson, a "pet whisperer" who wears a floppy winter hat every day of the year. Peterson said that the Gummy Monkeys, fat bouncy monkeys, and the Pygmy Moose, a smaller moose type, have to leave since they cannot stand the smell.

Each is heading in a different direction, some to the mountains and others to the Tangerine Forest's bottomless gravel pit.

The founder of the perfume company (Mr. Gazoon Height, a man who wears several watches) told us he only uses half of the tangerine, the rind. He said he follows all directions and laws. "You have it in your minds that I am destroying the tangerine forest," he said in a don't-accuse-me kind of voice.

We should have listened to Gazoon but we didn't. As we were talking to Ranger Ranger he let us check his bag and we found three tangerines. He then confessed that he has been the one taking the most tangerines. He has been searching in the night, looking for 200-foot tangerines with which to make perfume, to get back his wife, who has left him for Gazoon Height.

He understands his crime and wants to be forgiven.

Hopefully the forest will return to its wonderful state, but that means no more perfume if you want the Gummy Monkeys and Pygmy Mooses. It won't be easy, but with extra care it might work.

MYSTERY AND DECEIT IN THE TANGERINE FOREST

[In this workshop, students, ages 10–12, learned the secrets of great reporters by solving a mystery. The gummy bear trees has been dying and the tangerine forest is a mess. Why? Students interviewed the local tribes, government authorities, shady business owners, and the famous actors who were trying to save the forest. They then used the gathered information to write stories that are rich, vibrant, detail-filled, and interesting to read.]

The Mystery of the Tangerine Forest

by ALY ROBALINO

Age 11, Cabrillo Elementary

I stared up at the tall tangerine tree, inhaling the cool of the night. "Refreshing!" I thought through the rustling of the short breezes that rippled Dental Floss Lake. The moonlight created the bright glow from the dental floss that waved as gently as a mother rocking her baby to sleep.

It began when I got a call from a guy called Ranger Ranger. That's his name. Don't ask me. So I finally flipped my oak-brown hair behind my back and answered the small black phone that usually sat there staring at me. "Hello, this is the Detective Agency, Sasha at your service," I said into the phone.

"He-hello… I have a—*hic*—case t-to rep—*hic*—report," said a man's shaky voice. This man didn't sound tough or confident.

I replied, "Sir, Please tell me what your case is. Your name would help too." I sighed into the phone.

"My name is—*hic*—Ranger Ranger. I'm report—*hic*—ing a case of thievery. You see—*hic*—I live in the Tangerine Forest—*hic*—and all the tangerines are disappearing. It's causing all the animals to leave. Without the animals, the forest will die. The forest is my home! Please help—*hic*—me!"

Hmm… the Tangerine Forest… Ah! Yes! How could I have been so stupid? The Tangerine Forest is famous for its tangerines. "Ahh yes. The Tangerine Forest, you say?" I said a little more brightly. I'd always wanted to go there, but only workers or specific people can go in; perhaps this was my chance to actually go see the forest!

"Yes—*hic*—the Tangerine Forest…"

"Would you like me to come there to check things out? I mean, to see what's going on?" I asked, clutching the phone to my ear, turning my hand red and warm.

"Yes—*hic*—that would be great. You know the—*hic*—way?" he squeaked into the phone.

"Yes," I replied quickly.

"Let's—*hic*—meet by Dental Floss Lake in forty-five minutes. I'll let the guards—*hic*—know you're coming. Just take the path to the—*hic*—lake and follow the signs. Got it?"

"Yeah, okay, I'll be there. Bye."

"Bye." Click. Dashing out of the office, I grabbed my coat and pushed my gold-rimmed glasses up my nose. I went into my boss' office and told him where I was heading. I dashed out before he had a chance to reply, though I heard him murmur, "You really do take your job seriously."

The tires scrunched over the moss-green gravel. Backing up next to a tree covered in dark brown bark that was speckled with tangerines, I popped out of the rusty white pick-up truck, surveying the surroundings with my dark maroon eyes. I scanned the surroundings, seeing all the sights of Dental Floss Lake.

*   *   *

The lake glistened a light-mint, translucent color, and the bottom of the lake looked like a whole lot of toothpaste. I could also see strands of green, stringy plants in the lake. Oh yes, I must say it smelled refreshing, like a very strong Tic-Tac. I took a deep breath and straightened my jeans, adjusting the brown leather belt so I was comfortable, and tucked in my black shirt, as well. Yep, that's me, Sasha the semi-neat freak.

With all the nature noises and my mind thinking random thoughts, I didn't notice the man creeping up on me.

"—*hic*—"

Right then and there I could have sworn my heart stopped for a couple of seconds. I swerved my head around. A man of average height, with short black hair and dark brown eyes that looked tired and depressed, stood before me.

"You must be Ranger Ranger," I said, breathing rapidly from being startled and staring, wild-eyed, at him.

He hiccupped again and said, "Yes." I quickly remembered what I was here for and thought greedily that if I solved this mystery, I'd get a raise, or at least a bonus.

"Let's get down to business." For a whole hour he told me what was going on. Pygmy Moose were being affected because the Pygmy Moose eat the bark off the tangerine trees, and if the trees are dying, the Pygmy Moose will have nothing to eat.

Jelly monkeys were being affected the most. They are around three to three-and-a-half feet tall and are extremely fat. They have monkey-like faces, arms that are four feet long, and are excellent climbers. Something disturbing about them is that their body parts fall off, but they do grow back. The parts that fall off give the trees nutrients to help them live.

Ranger Ranger told me that the fragile ecosystem of the forest was being endangered by the thefts. I asked him if he had any enemies and he just paused and pressed his tongue to his cheek, making me suspicious. I repeated the question again because he was spacing out.

"Hello? Are you there?" I asked. "Oh for… do you *suspect* anyone?"

Ranger Ranger paused again and said simply, "Gazoon Height."

"Bless you?" I said giving him a "What? Can you repeat that?" look.

"Gazoon Height. He owns a big factory that creates love potions that are made from the rinds of the tangerines. The love potions are extremely popular. One taste and you'll fall in love at first sight with the next person you see. The love potion can be made with the tangerine rinds here."

"So you think it's him? No one else?"

"Yep."

It was time to pay a visit to Gazoon Height.

*   *   *

"Yes? What do you want? I'm very busy here!" growled a tall, muscular man with dark-brown hair speckled with a few lighter-colored strands.

"Sir, I'm Sasha from the Detective Agency. From now on you are a suspect in the Tangerine Forest Crime, until it is solved. Sorry," I said as he gave me a look that would kill if looks could kill.

"Look, I didn't choose you, actually. Ranger Rang…"

"*What*?! I'll kill him!" Gazoon Height bellowed. "When I'm

not busy," he growled.

"Umm... umm..." I stuttered, afraid he might attack me or that his heart would give out from anger. Gazoon Height's face was as red as if the blood in his cheeks were on the outside. "Please calm down," I said, stepping back and putting my hand on the dull greasy doorknob. Gazoon Height sighed, dropped his shoulders, and stepped back a step, his black shoes shining beneath the dim light.

"Sorry. I'm so busy these days. With this to put up with I'll never finish anything."

"Sorry, I'd just like to ask you a few questions. It won't take more than fifteen minutes of your time. Please?" I asked.

"Okay," said Gazoon Height. I took out a little brown notebook and a black pen I always kept in my pocket.

"How many tangerines are you allowed to take each week?"

"Twenty."

"How many tangerines do you take each week?"

"Twenty."

I scribbled onto the notebook and looked at him. "Ranger Ranger says more are being taken each week. The tangerines aren't able to grow back as fast as they're being taken."

Gazoon Height's face was turning red. I thought I might want to cut the questioning short.

"I don't take more than twenty tangerines a week," he growled.

"Okay... I get the point," I said nervously.

"Sorry," he grunted. "I know someone you might find useful. Pete Peterson, Animal Whisperer. He lives at 8377 Feciousious Avenue. Just to warn you though, he's a pretty strange guy. Seriously," he said, looking at me. I could have sworn he almost smiled at me, but since I'd spent barely ten minutes with him, it was hard to tell.

I said goodbye and my shoes squeaked along the linoleum floor, tracked with dirt. I wondered if they didn't have a janitor. They could use a better one if they did.

Slamming the car door, I turned the keys of my truck and pulled out of the small parking lot. I pulled up to the small driveway in a rather quiet part of town, 8377 Feciousious Ave. to be exact. The air didn't smell or taste as polluted as I would have thought. I got out my ID in case he asked why I had come, and I knocked on the door.

"Coming! I'll be there in a minute! Hold on!" hollered a voice from inside the house. I sort of envied the fact that he lived in a quiet suburban area.

Answering the door was a tall man who had blonde and brown hair and light skin that was red around the arms, sunburned no doubt. He wore a rather colorful hat that had drooping "ears."

His light blue eyes sparkled while he smiled a sort of charming smile. I could tell he would be a more likable person than Ranger Ranger or Gazoon Height, though if there's one thing I've learned throughout my life, it's to never judge a person by how he looks. Pete looked like he would be a little more normal. I was far from right.

"Hello. I'm Sasha from the Detective Agency. I heard you've spoken to the animals in the Tangerine Forest. Can you help me?

"That's me! Pete Peterson! Animal Whisperer at your service! I sure can tell you what they said, though I can't say it'll make a lot of sense."

Well, it was worth a shot. He invited me in and I glanced around his living room, which seemed to glow in the afternoon light.

Practically everything in the living room was white as well as neat.

"Okay," I said whipping out my pad and pen. "What exactly did they tell you that might be helpful?" I asked, looking at him softly.

"Well, the Jelly Monkeys were hard to talk to; almost all they can think about is tangerines and it's nearly impossible to get them to talk about anything else. While they did know who did it, they seemed reluctant to tell me. All they said was, 'The truth is in the bag.' I asked two or three of them and they said the same thing. I asked the Pygmy Moose, and do you know what? They said the same thing. They were all solemn though. If they gave the secret away, they'd feel terrible. They said it was to protect their only human friend," he said seriously.

As odd as he seemed, he had his serious moments. What I mean by odd is when I stared at him for a couple of seconds, he picked up a box of dog biscuits by his chair, smiled his charming grin, and asked, "You want one? They're actually pretty good."

I didn't want to be rude. He had given me the biggest clue someone could have given me. I said no thanks and I thanked him, saying I had a mystery to solve.

*   *   *

I knocked on Gazoon Height's office door and asked him if I could come in.

"Do you have a bag? If so, may I examine it?" I asked as soon as I was let in.

Gazoon Height just stared at me as if I had become insane. I probably should have explained first what I was doing.

I spotted a black leather bag by the foot of his desk. I snatched it up and said to him, "If I don't find what I think could be in here, then I know who it is and you will be cleared from the suspects list." I rooted through his bag, searching for the answer to this mystery. Pens, paper, notes, paper clips, pencils, some loose change, and a pack of sugar-free mint gum. Nope, not what I was looking for.

"Sorry about that. At least you are off the hook. You are no longer a suspect in this crime," I said to him.

I dashed out of the office and almost collided with another man, Ranger Ranger, who was just the man I wanted to see.

He carried a small red backpack that had a few loose strings. Before he could hiccup, let alone say sorry, I yanked off his backpack and ripped it open, wrapping my hand around a large plastic bag. Heavy as it was, I yanked it out. What did I see in there? About fifteen or twenty genuine Tangerine Forest tangerines.

"What do you have to say for yourself, Ranger Ranger?" I asked, smiling in triumph.

Ranger Ranger spilled everything. Poor guy, I think he was in shock.

"I-I-I was go-going to put the tangerines into Gazoon Height's bag so it looked like he stole them and he'd get the blame, and then I could get my girlfriend back and become rich so I could out-do Gazoon Height, so I'd be better than him! Ahggggg!" He screamed and dashed off in terror.

Well, now his case of annoying hiccups is gone. The animals will slowly return, and it looks like I'll hand the rest over to the police. They'll have him in jail in no time at all. I smirked to myself and decided to visit Dental Floss Lake one more time, just to sniff the minty air one last time before I go.

POET-FREE WORKSHOP

[*Poet-Free: Free the Poet in You! was an introduction to poetry taught by Michelle Ryan in the fall of 2005. Students learned about language, rhyme, metaphor, and other poetic tools. They also had the opportunity to free-write and share the results aloud with their classmates.*]

A Hat

by SABINE DAHI
Age 8, Clarendon Elementary

A hat fell off a cliff
it fell on a child's head
and fell off the child's head.

[*Poet-Free: Free the Poet in You!* was an introduction to poetry taught by Michelle Ryan in the Fall of 2005. Students learned about language, rhyme, metaphor, and other poetic tools. They also had the opportunity to free-write and share the results aloud with their classmates.]

Sound

by MAYA CHATTERJEE
Age 8, Clarendon Elementary

You can hear anything—talking, barking, meowing—and when it's there, you can almost always hear shouting. But what I like to hear most is music. Soft, peaceful music. I can hear wind, water, gurgling, dripping, television, storms, spinning chairs, scraping chalk. I can also hear computers and humming. I wish I could hear chocolate, cake, cookies—oh,oh,oh!—it would smell so sweet.

POET-FREE WORKSHOP

[Poet-Free: Free the Poet in You! was an introduction to poetry taught by Michelle Ryan in the Fall of 2005. Students learned about language, rhyme, metaphor, and other poetic tools. They also had the opportunity to free-write and share the results aloud with their classmates.]

It is a Tree

by CHRIS DANISON
Age 9, Alvarado Elementary

It looks like
blood and gore.
It sounds like
the scream of a dying man.
It smells like
rotten eggs.
It feels like
burning oil.
It tastes like
nuclear waste.
It is a
violent, stupid
tree.

POET-FREE WORKSHOP

[Poet-Free: Free the Poet in You! was an introduction to poetry taught by Michelle Ryan in the Fall of 2005. Students learned about language, rhyme, metaphor, and other poetic tools. They also had the opportunity to free-write and share the results aloud with their classmates.]

Magic Box

by MAYA CHATTERJEE
Age 8, Clarendon Elementary

I will put in the box…
A cat with three legs,
Some purple caterpillars,
A dog made out of steel,
A horse made out of wind,
A bunny made out of tulips,
A fox that has blue stripes,
A human, made out of magic.

POET-FREE WORKSHOP

[Poet-Free: Free the Poet in You! was an introduction to poetry taught by Michelle Ryan in the Fall of 2005. Students learned about language, rhyme, metaphor, and other poetic tools. They also had the opportunity to free-write and share the results aloud with their classmates.]

Mystery Figure

by CHRIS DANISON

Age 9, Alvarado Elementary

I am so strong, I lift boulders.
I am so weak that I stumble
under the weight of my hat.
I am so graceful I stand on one toe.
I am so clumsy I stick my thumb in my eye.
Who am I?

[Poet-Free: Free the Poet in You! was an introduction to poetry taught by Michelle Ryan in the Fall of 2005. Students learned about language, rhyme, metaphor, and other poetic tools. They also had the opportunity to free-write and share the results aloud with their classmates.]

Monarch Butterfly

by CASEY ROOS

Age 11, St. Cecilia School

Dancing fairly above the trees,
born in meadows, flies over seas
lives in Mexico, flies to Monterrey
caught in a web, opens its broken wing.
Tries to fly
stuck
about to die
same fate as the well-known fly
spider's retreat
winning relief,
saved
by a homosapien.

[*In a collaboration that's become a tradition, two freshman classes from MetWest joined us for six Fridays in a row at the beginning of the 2005–06 school year to write, edit, and publish a collection of short stories. This year, the stories were based on life experiences.*]

My Driving Lessons

by RAY PEREZ
Age 15, MetWest High School

"**B**eat ya," I said to my little brother, Ezekiel, as I won the race.

"Man, you cheated," he said. We were playing my favorite game, Need for Speed Underground 2. It's a racing game where you create your own cars and race them.

"Let's turn on the Raider game," I said. "I bet you that the Raiders are winning."

After we finished playing, we turned off the car game and turned on the TV. It was the Raiders against the Chargers, and we were winning, as usual, twenty-one to seven.

"I told you that the Raiders were winning," I said to my brother. Suddenly we heard a knock on our front door.

"It's uncle Alex," said my little brother.

"Angel, open the door," said a voice behind the door.

I opened the door and I saw my uncle Alex, my aunt Erica, and my little cousin Anglo. My cousin is two years old and he can talk and walk. He is around two feet tall, has long brown hair, brown eyes, and light skin, and is very skinny. My uncle Alex is about seven feet tall, and light-skinned, has brown eyes, always wears a black hat, and always has on a lot of jewelry. As soon as I opened the door, my cousin said, "Ezekiel."

"Lolo," my brother said, using my little cousin's nickname.

"What's up, Angel?" asked my uncle Alex.

"What's up, Alex?" We were all excited because we hadn't seen each other in a long time. We all sat down on my couch and started watching the Raiders game.

"So, what have you been up to?" said my uncle.

"Nothing much, just watching the game and playing racing games," I replied.

"Yeah?" said my uncle. "Do you like cars?"

"They're all right," I said.

"Have you ever driven a car before?" asked my uncle.

"No," I responded.

"Do you want to?" asked my uncle.

"Yes," I said.

I did not think that he was serious, but when I saw him talking to my mother about it and she agreed, I was very excited. I pretty much jumped up and down and couldn't shut up. I asked a million questions about when and where I was going to drive. I never thought that I would learn how to drive at age thirteen.

The night before I was going to start, I was nervous because I'd never driven a car before. I couldn't sleep because I kept thinking about what would happen if I crashed, or wondering if I would go to jail if a cop caught me driving without a license. I called my uncle and told him that I couldn't sleep because I was nervous. He said that it was up to me if I wanted to drive, and he also explained that we were going to go to a place where there are rarely any cars and no cops, so there would be little chance of anything happening. He also said that I shouldn't worry about it because he trusts me. That gave me a lot of confidence. After I talked to him, I finally calmed down and was able to sleep.

As soon as I woke up, I got ready and waited outside for my uncle to come and pick me up. I was looking for a very old, broken-everything red Camero. I was looking all over the place. I kept hearing a car beeping. It was a brand new 2006 black Lexus SC 430 convertible with new twenty-inch rims. I looked at it for a long time. Then it honked again. I looked to see who was driving the car and I saw my uncle. I was very surprised, but I ran up to the car and got in.

"Where did you get the car?" I asked my uncle.

"From this car dealership place by my house," he said.

While we were in the car heading to the place where I was going to drive, we talked about what to do and what not to do. For example, he said I should learn how to park, stop at a red light, turn both ways, reverse, and drive at the speed limit.

We drove to Bay Farm Island in Alameda, and from there we drove up to the shoreline. That was where I was going to drive. It was a very nice place. There was a beach to the right of it. There were brand new streets. It was a lonely and quiet place. There was a beautiful view of the skyline of San Francisco. There were only a few cars in that area that day.

"Are you ready?" asked my uncle.

"Yeah, are you?" I said excitedly.

I checked my mirrors, took the emergency brake off, and asked, "What do I do now?"

He said, "Just start driving."

I turned on the car and started driving. At first I was nervous, and I was going very slowly. Then I came to a stop sign and hit the brakes too soon. The stop sign was ten feet in front of the car, and I felt stupid. My uncle told me to calm down, relax, and not worry. He said that I was doing fine. I turned on the radio because it relaxes me and calms me down. Then I turned left and went around the block several times until I got the hang of driving and stopping at the signs. I decided to go straight until I saw an empty parking lot. Then I turned right into the lot and I tried parking; it took me a long time, but eventually I learned how to park and reverse. While I was parked, we talked about what all the traffic signs meant and what I needed to do when I came across one. We went over all the buttons and things in the car. For example, he taught me how to use the windshield wipers, the emergency blinking signal, and the headlights, and where the gas gauge is so that I would be aware of how much gas I had and would know when it was time to put more in the car. I pulled out of the parking lot and drove to a nearby restaurant, and we ate. Well, it wasn't really a restaurant. It was Carl's Junior.

After we ate we went to the shoreline of the beach. I switched seats with my uncle and started to drive again. I stepped on the gas, and I was speeding. I started to lose control, so I hit the brakes. My uncle took the wheel and I was scared. But we got through that little scene, and that was it for the day.

When we finally got home, my brother and mother came out to meet me and to hear how it went. I was very excited and told them about everything that happened. I told them that I wanted to drive again as soon as possible.

My uncle came every other weekend to take me out to drive.

Every time was a different experience, and I always learned something new. I learned how to drive on the street with other cars and not to be nervous around a lot of vehicles. I learned how to parallel park on the street and how to make a three point turn. The only thing I haven't done yet is go on the freeway, and that will not be for a while because my mother thinks it is too much for me right now. She says that the cars go very fast on the freeway and I need to be more experienced. My uncle also told me about the maintenance that I need to do on the car to keep it running in good condition. He said I should have an oil change every 3,000 miles and that I should check the oil and the air in the tires every week. I need to wash the car when it gets dirty and make sure that all the lights are working properly. There is a lot of maintenance to do on a car that I didn't know about.

I feel grown up and more responsible about many things now. I think that I changed a lot from learning how to drive. I learned that I should give everything a chance before I judge it.

[*In a collaboration that's become a tradition, two freshman classes from MetWest joined us for six Fridays in a row at the beginning of the 2005–06 school year to write, edit, and publish a collection of short stories. This year, the stories were based on life experiences.*]

Thai Quest

by TIEN ORTMAN

Age 15, MetWest High School

We were riding elephants in the Thai rain forest. As we walked it was very bumpy for us because we were on rocks and shallow water. I was thinking that I was tired from the ride. I was also thinking about how I was going to eat a lot at the camp.

We were on the second day of the trek in Thailand. We were about to stop in a village, and as we came near we started to see people around. Kids were running around and there was a woman washing clothes. There were monkeys around us that I heard in the background. There were also many tall plants of many colors and sizes. We were so high up on the elephants. It was like being on top of a Hummer, but the elephant had more power. The sun was high and bright, but we were shaded by the vast canopy of the rainforest. I was thinking that I needed to get a hat because there was lots of sun.

We got off the bumpy elephant ride and saw the elephants leave. I have always liked the way they walk. They are giant swaying animals with great balance.

When I looked around, I saw lots of huts and trees. The trees were so green because of the rainfall. It seemed like they were ever-greens. The air was so clean there that it was like having a natural air filter.

We were looking around the village and I saw two huts that were off to the side. They turned out to be our place to sleep. It looked like the huts were made of large bamboo shoots with a ceiling of hard material. The mats we slept on were made of crushed bamboo. The bamboo mats were not soft, but they were easy to sleep on. I put my stuff down and started to wander around the village. At the top of the village, I saw a shrine to their gods. The dolls were made of lots of plants, unlike modern-day dolls in the US. The paint was made of natural dyes and native materials. The shrine also had lots of other items near the bottom. Some pictures of people—perhaps passed relatives. There was a group of people that came and started praying as the sun fell. When that happened, I moved out of the way.

I continued to walk around, and I saw a run-down school-house and a volleyball court. I started to play with the kids. We couldn't understand each other, but we were able to play nonethe-less. We played volleyball with a hacky sack. The court had a net like the ones we have in some schools. The hacky sack is made of woven grass and shoots from plants. The Thai kids were better than me at putting it over the net with their feet, but I had fun anyway. You should see them; they are so good that they can get the sack over the net like it is a volleyball. The first time I tried, I could hardly hit it, and the Thai kids started to laugh at me.

Then the sun went down and we went to the campfire by our huts. We started eating dinner. For dinner we had green curry with chicken and native plants. The green curry is the hottest of the curries, but it is still good.

After dinner there was a group of villagers that wanted to hear the kind of music we listen to. I started to sing "Baby Got Back," and my aunt started dancing. I sang really badly but the people did not care. I don't think they cared about the fact that I was a bad singer and that my aunt could not dance. The way she danced was so funny. After that we went to bed. It was so peaceful. There was no sound and no light but the light from the moon.

In the morning, I woke up before everyone else and went outside, where I saw our guide making breakfast. We had eggs and fruit with a little toast. Afterwards, there was a bunch of villagers that came to sell us things. We bought a couple of hats. The hats were so colorful with red, green, blue, and a touch of purple; they were great. My Aunt laughed at the hat I had on. It looked like a cross between a fez and a jester's hat. We also got some water-bottle holders. They have a long cloth string for a shoulder strap. They still work, too. After that we hiked all day and got on the truck to leave. That was the most fun I have ever had.

On the truck I thought about how much less the people in the rainforest have than we do. They get new toys and other things once a month if they are lucky. The men that are in their twenties go into the cities and get stuff for the people. The toys that they had were either made from wood and cloth or worn out. I saw a doll with no hands or head. They had so much less.

[*For several years now, 826 has helped work with Everett Middle School to produce their school newspaper, the* Straight-Up News. *Students involved can be found in the Everett Writers' Room each week writing investigative reports and feature articles, drawing comics, and performing interviews. The best of these pieces can be both topical and pithy.*]

Everett Celebrates Day of Peace

by KARLA HERNANDEZ

Age 13, Everett Middle School

Everett Middle School celebrates things every day, but in January we celebrate with a special ceremony called the Day of Peace.

Seventh-grade student Marlene Olmedo was asked about her favorite part of the Day of Peace, and she said, "My favorite part is when everybody says, 'Happy Peace Day!'"

When asked why he thought the Day of Peace is important, seventh grader Roberto Hernandez said, "Because everybody celebrates the Day of Peace with family and friends and everybody is happy."

Teachers and students do a lot of work together to celebrate Peace Day, but the most important part of the ceremony is when the students and teachers say "Happy Peace Day" to each other.

[For several years now, 826 has helped work with Everett Middle School to produce their school newspaper, the Straight-Up *News. Students involved can be found in the Everett Writers' Room each week writing investigative reports and feature articles, drawing comics, and performing interviews. The best of these pieces can be both topical and pithy.]*

The Secret of Blockbuster Hits

by GUILLERMO GONZALEZ

Age 12, Everett Middle School

WHAT makes a blockbuster? A blockbuster movie can contain comedy or romance—a lot of movies are based on these subjects! There can also be a lot of action in a blockbuster, such as fighting, helicopter jumping, and other stuff like that. A blockbuster has to contain an introduction about what is happening in the character's life, like what they want or what they like to do. Some movies, like sequels, begin with a bang and then introduce new characters in addition to the old ones.

After this, the conflict is introduced. There is often danger and suspense involved in the conflict that lead to a point where the main character or characters reach a life-changing decision. An example of this is "Spiderman 2." Just when Peter Parker has enough to worry about, they do something else to make him blow his top, like put him down or threaten his family. All hope seems to be lost and they believe they have won, but then he realizes through his internal conflict (internal conflict is when a character has a struggle within himself, in his head, and has to make a decision) that if he does not make the right decision, everyone will be doomed. This is the part that leaves you hanging.

The next part is the climax. The climax is the part when the hero has found a way to defeat the monster in his head and will now try to defeat the villain, whoever it may be (it could be a dragon or an old friend). The point is, the hero will have to try, try, try!!! Only one character will succeed, and guess who it is? If you guessed hero, you were right! People respect heroes because they think, "He was cool. He just saved the world."

Then comes the falling point. This is when the conflict is resolved, everything is finishing, and the credits come on.

Juliet Snowden, 39, is a screenwriter in Los Angeles who has written the blockbuster, "The Boogeyman." She says that you can't just sit down to write a blockbuster. "If Hollywood knew what made a blockbuster, somebody would be getting really rich," she says. "You can increase your chances by 'packaging' a movie, which means getting a well-known director and famous actors, but it's still not guaranteed. The public decides what a blockbuster is." She talked about how the blockbuster, "The Terminator," came from a very small idea. The director just thought of a robot stepping out of a flame, and the rest of the movie followed.

Snowden says she's been writing since she was about the age of Everett Middle School students, but that writing is still very difficult. She is now working on the script for a remake of Alfred Hitchcock's famous movie, "The Birds." "I think it will be a blockbuster, but I could be wrong!"

"I've found that the only way I can work is to work on something that's interesting to me," says Ms. Snowden, who works with her husband, who is also a screenwriter. "If we don't think it's cool, the people who watch it won't think it's cool, either!"

AT-LARGE SUBMISSIONS

Receiving an at-large submission is like receiving a birthday gift. We live for this. If you are between the ages of 6 and 18, we want your words. The section that follows represents a world of children and young adults writing on their own, in their homes, under their trees, with their best friends, about their enemies, being young, their favorite foods, magic, a horse. Happy birthday to us and keep them coming!

Please send your submission to:

The 826 Quarterly
826 Valencia Street
San Francisco, CA 94110

For submission guidelines, please visit the *Quarterly* page on our website: www.826valencia.org/writing/quarterlyguide.

Flashbulb

by CHRISTINA JONES

Age 17, College Preparatory High School

The nail had stabbed below the palm, piercing cleanly through the wrist. For a long pause they said nothing, and in the quiet Alexa could hear the in, out, in of Dillon's breaths. He looked unusually calm, his face white and expressionless like a paper plate. He was staring at his arm but his eyes were wide without understanding, as if he couldn't believe the sight of the copper nail coming through the flesh. Somewhere off in the distance a dog barked. Dillon yanked his arm free. The nail slid away cleanly, leaving behind a prick of blood on his wrist. Alexa swallowed hard.

"Dillon, your shoes weren't tied, were they? Don't you blame me. That's your fault. Not mine. Mom's gonna be angry, so angry, because she always tells you not to trip over your laces, but of course you had to fall on the plywood and get hurt, and now she won't let us have pizza for dinner and—"

The spot of blood was trickling into a larger flow, watercolor red, streaking down Dillon's arm. Alexa blinked. She took his hand and pressed her fingers to his wrist, pushing hard into the flesh, but the blood continued to leak, sneaking through the cracks between her fingers. She squeezed harder, trying to plug up the wound, and still the blood came, bright, like the cherry slurpies Dillon drank on hot Saturday afternoons. Alexa squeezed her eyes shut.

Please, make it stop.

Why had they come to the field? Better yet, why had *Dillon* come? Hadn't she told him not to come? He didn't listen. He never listened. Dillon always tagged along, ruining her fun—whining, crying, forgetting to tie his shoes or wear sunscreen—making it her fault when he scrapped his knees or got sunburned. Mom said Alexa needed to watch out for her little brother because he was only four years old, but Alexa didn't want to take care of him. She was nine and much too old for Dillon. She didn't want him along. She wished he'd disappear, like when he'd stayed hidden in the closet for hours after she'd wordlessly abandoned their hide-and-seek game. Served him right. This served him right, too. Maybe he'd finally learn to leave her alone.

Dillon hiccupped out a sob.

Alexa opened her eyes and glanced down. The blood had smeared onto her skirt, staining the white cloth. She looked at her brother. His hand was turning robin-egg-blue. She'd seen that color once before, in the skin of a dead chick lying beside the road. Only a few days old, it had fallen out of its nest, and when she found the bird it was bloated, still featherless, its black-bean eyes staring at the sky.

"Run," she whispered.

Dillon cried louder. She grabbed his shoulder and tugged him, but he remained on his knees.

"*Run!*"

She pulled harder. Dillon stumbled to his feet. She let go of her grip, and as they ran she counted time to the pulse of her heart in her ears. *One-one-thousand. Two-one-thousand. Three-one-thousand. Four-* When they arrived at the front of the house Mom and Grandma were already standing at the door, yelling words Alexa didn't understand, and she wondered how they had known to come outside so quickly, how they'd known Dillon was in trouble. Then Alexa realized that she was screaming, nonsense sounds burning from her throat, as she and Dillon stumbled up the steps, up, up, up to Mom and Grandma and home and safety.

Mom gathered Dillon into her arms and moments later Alexa heard car doors slamming, saw a cloud of dust rising as they drove off to the hospital where the doctors would make everything all right. As the car disappeared down the road Alexa remained on the porch for a long while, listening to the dry chirps of crickets from the field, trying to quiet her tears. Grandma placed a hand on her shoulder. When she stopped crying they went into the house and turned on the TV set, but even Bugs Bunny couldn't make Alexa forget the image of the nail sticking through Dillon's wrist. During the commercials she pressed her knuckles against her eyelids and tried to block out the memories from that afternoon.

Later that night, when Mom arrived back from the hospital, she came into Alexa's room and told her that she had been a good girl, so mature and grownup, for bringing Dillon quickly home. Alexa wanted to say thank you, but as she tried to get out the words her voiced cracked.

Mom came to the bed and pulled her into a hug, whispering over and over into her hair, "Everything's going to be all right," but Alexa cried harder. She knew it wasn't true; everything wouldn't be all right, not ever again, because whenever she'd closed her eyes she knew she'd see the field in her mind, the dirt mixing with Dillon's blood, blending into black.

Faking It

by LIZ BENEFIEL

Age 17, The Marin School

T hey were swarming. Millions of the creatures were born up on white wings, swooping into the broad arm of empty air. They made no sound. Helen could feel their restless wind down in her ribs, deeper even, and loneliness made it somehow bearable.

This is what Helen imagines whenever she listens to Tchaikovsky. In the *1812 Overture*, they dive deep into a paprika canyon and emerge when the bells cry out, their eyes red with glory. In *Sleeping Beauty* they are flying very low over a lake where no land is visible. First it is two, dipping and bobbing over each other, until a wave of them surge from the water and crest so high their blood shines in the sun. And when it is *Marche Slave*, they are all grey, zipping through a narrow stone quarry, their eyes black onyx, spinning down into the water, which reflects only clouds.

What could be more pleasant than this, listening to rapturous music on an airplane in an upright seat, the moisture sucked from every orifice? Helen could not imagine a greater joy, other than dying. The most delicious part of life, Helen thinks to herself, is anticipation. There is no act so pleasurable that the waiting for the act does not surpass it.

Now it is Brahms and his lullabies. With Brahms, Helen feels the dark fire inside of her spread like a drop of ink in water. She brushes her collarbone with her fingertips, seeing them as paint-brushes of her own hair, leaving iridescent trails over her nubile, tender flesh.

Oh, but she is thirty–five! Thirty–five years young, married for seven, in remission for six. She would not have married him if she knew she was going to live. If only she could be thirteen again and revel in it, if she could be young but still know what she knows now. So many beautiful young men yearned for her then, but would they now, with her support hose and orthopedic shoes and the embarrassing lingerie that her husband bought for her? She wishes she could go back and age well, apply moisturizer and wear sunblock. She wishes she quit smoking twenty years ago, though of course it was fun then. And here, out the window, is an ocean, reflecting back the sun's white eye.

"Coffee, miss?" the stewardess asks her. Helen shakes her head, a smile banded tight on her face. The flight attendant lingers for another second to ask the person (an ugly man) on Helen's left. She thinks of how the girl—the stewardess—is tired, such a joyless job, and she wants to tell her everything she knows to prevent her from this disease of growing old and dying. It does not matter much now. She listens to Bach. What a bland composer! But his fugues enthrall her: This is music with an eye of death in it. When listening to them she feels clouds, fat and grey, supporting her like a cold, wet bed. She wants nothing more but for the last note to remain, to linger like the taste of a good fruit or a lover, in the air forever, so she can fall and lose herself in it.

There! Her Mr. Paris is waiting at the gate. His eyes are moist and touched with sadness, and Helen wishes immediately to walk back into the safe womb of the plane, explain the mistake and take a return trip. He is smiling. His teeth are slightly grey and a pouch of fat has established its place around his middle. She doesn't want her face to fall. Helen hugs Mr. Paris, almost with urgency. The stirrings of some song awaken inside her.

"Hello, Miss Laurence," he says, and she blushes to herself. She is glad she has not told him of her marriage (the gods would not approve) and her new name, Mrs. Menelaos. How Mediterranean.

Mr. Paris looks at her critically—she is herself, but not quite. She was more herself then, but now, with waxy yellow skin and banana-colored teeth, and putty-colored makeup gathering in the lines around her eyes. He remembers her smoking in bed, her ashtray-flavored kisses. He used to say he loved her for her mind.

Thank Christ I quit, he thinks. He puts his hand on the small of her back.

"You look good," he says, and watches her blush. A smile oozes on her face like a lazy egg yolk.

"No, I don't," she says. She takes out a handkerchief and coughs into it.

"I reserved us a room at the Four Seasons," he says. "Are you all right?"

"Yes."

"Do you need to take some medicine, or—"

"No, no." She looks at the floor. She looks into his eyes. "I'm starting treatment next week." (How could she explain to him that she has not told anyone about her symptoms, neither her husband nor her doctor nor her therapist nor her friends—and that she does not plan to?) Sensing some isolation coming between them, she takes his hand.

There is a small pause, a beat where Mr. Paris inhales through his nose and looks at her shoes. He hopes that her feet are the same. When they took a bath together at his parent's house she lifted up her foot involuntarily, and he felt everything inside him shrink until he was infinitely small, a tiny dot, sensation compressed into oblivion.

Mr. Paris was certain of his death. Only years later, as he went through his divorce, would he idly flip through a book of poetry and understand what had happened.

Mr. Paris brushes her shoulder with his hand.

"Do you have any bags?" he asks. "Anything else," he gestures to her purse, "that you have with you?"

"No," she says. He raises an eyebrow.

"Okay. My car is in the parking lot. Let's go."

Helen sees him as he was then, fifteen (fifteen?!) years back. She was a better student than he was. He never found out about her affair with the provost (who was better), which made her anger at his infidelity seem justified. She has never felt guilty about it until now.

Mr. Paris begins walking, his arm crooked across her shoulders. She walks slightly in front of him, her head tilted down. She wants to run, with him or alone, away from this airport terminal with its conditioned air and fluorescent lights and crowds of people whose only bond is mutual loneliness. She sees a young couple kissing and a fire of shame burns brightly on her cheeks. She needs a cigarette.

"Will you kiss me?" she asks, turning her body to block his. He frowns.

"Are you sure?"

"Don't worry!" She puts her hands on his hips. "My husband will never find out, I promise," she says, and lunges for him. Their lips graze each other before he grabs her arms and pushes her away.

"Your husband?" he asks.

They ride to the hotel in silence. In Helen's mind they are talking about their mutual friends, who they've kept in contact with, anything to keep them from thinking about themselves, about each other. Mr. Paris is rubbing her back and smiling, and Helen is smoking a Gauloise, or rolling a Drum, like she used to do in high school before she met him. He is playing his old jazz records in the CD player (somehow) and they are pretending that she has not been married for the last ten years.

Mr. Paris is imagining himself in the car with his ex-wife and his baby daughter, seven years ago, when they were married. He is talking to his wife about finances, about being fiscally responsible, about how to properly use credit cards and avoid debt and he mentions Helen for some reason, he doesn't remember why. She is not jealous; she never was, but he wonders if that was the happiest time of his life: when he had a child and a wife, both of whom he could control, and a past which he knew and could tell anybody about if he wanted. He is so absorbed he almost misses the turn for the Four Seasons. A man in a black coat takes his key from him. Another man in a black coat opens the passenger door. Airless music emanates from the speakers.

"It's Boccherini's *Menuet*," Helen says to herself, and Mr. Paris doesn't quite hear her. He makes a low noise in his throat and raises his eyebrows to indicate that she should repeat herself. "Boccherini," she says, "Boccherini's *Menuet*." He nods as if he understands, which he doesn't.

Mr. Paris takes care of the reservations. He is charming and effusive to the boy behind the counter, who laughs at his jokes and avoids making eye contact with Helen. When the transaction is through, Mr. Paris takes a twenty dollar bill out of his back pocket and drops it in front of the boy. He walks away before he can gauge a reaction. Helen looks back and sees the boy staring after them, his glasses white from the chandelier's reflection, his expression unreadable. The elevator is full of people, most younger than them, and they squeeze into opposite parts of the elevator.

"What floor?" a young boy with wet-looking hair asks them.

"Sixteen," Helen replies. The boy presses the button with his thumb.

Helen undresses quickly, facing the window, which is open. The breeze makes her skin feel almost alive. A pool of blue light spills onto the bed, with its high mattress and half-dozen pillows, the top cover a green-and-orange paisley. She has some trouble getting onto the bed. First, the pillows have to be removed, and then the top cover, and then the golden felt slip with its smell of perfumed violence. A tremor passes through her, then recedes, like a wave breaking over a rock. She does not want to look at his body. He takes the smooth plane of his hand and traces it along her collarbone to her jaw. When they kiss, she tastes his toothpaste and smells his cologne.

His hands feel like sandpaper dragging against her skin. His lips are two slugs battling over parts of her body. She cannot bear this torture, yet she feels nothing. He kills whatever he touches until she is numb everywhere, dead, save for what she can see: the ceiling, with its minute grooves and ridges and a fan, turning lazily on its axis.

When it is over, he kisses her and goes to the bathroom. She turns her head to the window, so she will not have to watch. A bird sings something that sounds almost like joy. She sits up, slowly, and walks to the window, holding a sheet up to her chest.

Mr. Paris stays in the bathroom for a long time looking at himself in the mirror. He wonders about his life. He walks to the shower and turns off the faucet. The door opens and a cold draft of air launches itself into the room.

"What are you doing?" he asks. Helen is naked, both feet over the edge of the window sill, her body supported by her frail arms. She looks like a mad woman. He can see clearly the web of stretch marks spreading out from her hips, the saggy folds of skin on her back, and he knows that the people outside can see her surgery scar, a pink and poreless gash, stretched like a snake across her torso. This is a scar he has kissed.

"Helen," he says again. He would rather be anywhere else right now. He would rather be with his divorce lawyer or his wife's divorce lawyer or drinking with the annoying secretary at work. He wants her to disappear, he wants her to never call him, he does not want the other people to see. "Helen," he repeats.

The well of sadness expands inside her at the sound of his voice. On the sidewalk, a boy and girl have stopped playing to look up at her. The mother is still talking on the phone. Nobody else is paying attention.

"Please don't do it," Mr. Paris says, but Helen does not hear him anymore. She looks at the children, their eyes wide with awe, their mouths open in silent tandem. Helen waves.

Unbearable Pain

by JOHN FERNANDEZ
Age 15, Balboa High School

My father was trying to open the new box of cigarettes. His lips were moving from right to left. When he finally fished out a cigarette he covered his lighter. He had to flick the lighter four times to get a flame. My dad was mesmerized by the dancing flames as they got closer to the cigarette. As he took a puff off the cigarette, the pained look on his face relaxed into a smile.

When my mom sees the smoke floating in the air, she gets a fan and fans the smoke away. The smell of the smoke is so strong that it makes me want to open all the windows; my mom leaves the room when she sees my dad smoking in the house. Sometimes I hear the voices of my dad and my grandmother arguing, then I see my dad walking outside the house with a frustrated face. My father takes out a cigarette, his face frustrated, then calm.

Before my dad smoked he was successful at school. He was even a great basketball player. Basketball was his passion and kept him away from smoking. If he didn't get good grades then he wouldn't be able to play basketball, and going to school every day helped him stay away from drugs. My grandfather was the one who motivated him by going to his basketball games, always supporting him. This is what kept my dad away from cigarettes.

But then my grandfather couldn't go to the basketball games because he was always working. When my grandfather couldn't attend his basketball games, my dad started to hang out with the wrong crowd. This is when he started smoking and started to not care about grades or anything else. Then my dad dropped out of high school and he always had fights with his mom.

Every time I see my dad's hands picking up the cigarette, I feel like throwing his pack of cigarettes down the toilet so he won't be able to find them. When I see my dad smoking, I feel sad and ask him, "Why do you smoke? Don't you know it's bad for you?" But he turns away and never gives me an answer. The smoke goes into my lungs and when I think about it, I feel like opening all the windows. The fumes make my lungs feel brittle, and I gasp for air.

My sister cries sometimes, because she doesn't want to see our dad smoking. She throws away the cigarettes, so that my dad won't find them. She doesn't like to imagine my dad suffering from the cigarettes, either. Every day my sister and I try and try to help in any way we can to stop my dad's addiction to cigarettes.

I find ways to occupy my dad to keep him from smoking. I make my dad laugh, to see his eyes closing and his mouth wide open. He tries to hide the laughter. He seems to be happier when he isn't smoking. I beg him to stop. Every time I see his sad face, and his rough hands trying to pick up the cigarette, I feel a hammering on my heart.

Douglass Keith LaBean I

by ROZ LABEAN

Age 17, Wallenberg High School

A young girl of six sits,
Her legs folded under her,
Her hazel eyes gazing upward
At her grandfather,
Sitting in the deep mahogany chair
With the base which he welded with his own
    two hands.

She looks down at those hands,
Shaking yet strong,
Telling endless stories
Of hardworking hours.

The girl's long blonde hair
Flows down her back.
Her soft and milky hands
Are neatly folded in her lap.

His frizzy gray beard
Tapers off a couple inches
Below his chin,
His forearms covered in old tattoos,
Each one telling a story—
An eagle, from when he joined the Army,
In a fading blue dye.

He tells me of his years working in the shipyards
As a welder,
His days stationed in Germany,
And the lessons he learned on the journey.

He taps his foot and sings along
To a Johnny Cash song on the cassette player.
"I went down, down, down,
And the flames went higher."

His eyes look tired and worn
And his smile is soft at the edges.
He pats his granddaughter's head
And slowly stands up, his face in a grimace,
From the stiffness of sitting too long.

The little girl gets up quickly,
Gets on her tip toes,
And wraps her small arms around his legs,
Only able to reach his waist,
Her neck cold against his metal belt buckle.

She grins up at him,
Giving his legs one more squeeze,
Before she lets go
And runs off to play.

Clouds I

by AUSTIN LEWIS

Age 13, Vista Learning Collaborative

The green grass tickles
the back of my legs.
A butterfly flits in the flowers.
A bee buzzes lazily along, stopping now and again.
The clouds roll by, unhurried,
Like an elephant that has all the time in the world.
A face here, a horse there,
Now a crocodile.
Now a bird,
A fish, a ship.
Things all shapes and sizes,
A big mural in the sky.

My Yellow

by STORMY KELLY

Age 16, Balboa High School

The cars were rushing around the single-story
yellow apartment complex.
I stood in the middle, barefoot,
surrounded by my yellow,
while the soft, deep grass molded to my foot.
There he was, standing ten feet away—
my daddy is with me and today we'll play,
not knowing in three years he won't be there.
It's not like I'd miss him
because you can't miss something
if it was never there.
Before I could have noticed
the red water balloon left my five-year-old hand.
It missed
but it was so close.
I'll always be close,
but never really there,
just like him,

standing tall as a street light,
skinny as a street light,
bright as a street light,
as the balloon landed, it splashed,
so close but not there.
And there was my hair
not dancing like normal.
The wind was the music to my hair
when it was long,
golden brown and flowing behind me
as I ran away from him.
He had a green water balloon
in his forty-year-old hand.
Sure the water, in thirty seconds,
would meet my purple plaid dress,
what a mess.

Yellow Wall

by JASMIN RIVERA
Age 9, Longfellow School

It is a rainy day.
I cannot
go outside
and play with my friends.

You! Yellow wall,
I will wait for you
to tell me a story
until the sun comes out.

Auntie E.

by VAOSA LOGOVII

Age 16, Balboa High School

I t all started when Auntie E.'s father passed away. It was really hard for us to handle her because she had been with him ever since she was born. I mean, he'd spoiled the hell out of her. She started crying and then everybody started crying. She had long-ass hair, down to there, if I can put it that way. When he died, she started cutting it and cutting it until she became a lesbian.

Auntie E. and her mother fought day and night because her mother didn't want her to be a lesbian. Because she said it's a sin against God. Everybody else, we all respect Auntie E.

Auntie E. walks like a man. She sags her pants and when she walks she goes sideways. And she makes her own self look good. She has no shame about herself. She has black, short hair, a pierced lip, and pierced eyebrow, too. Her legs are so hairy, you don't want to look. She tells everybody she wants to change her gender. Some people say "no," some say "yes." Most of the people say that they don't care—it's not their body, their problem, and whatever she wants to be or do, we will support her. We will always respect it.

Because she's big and she talks a lot, we started calling her Miss

Piggy. Miss Piggy doesn't like being called "her" or "she." You can only call her a "he" or "him." She really thinks that she is a real man, but inside those pants it's all one-hundred-percent woman. But we respect what she wants us to call her. She told me, "Don't get it twisted she is not a she, she is a he." She, I mean he, told me he doesn't want to do what the girls are doing—he wants to stay out late at night. One night Miss Piggy stayed out hella late. When he came home, he was drunk, with short hair. Miss Piggy's mother was not in a good mood. She was waiting, with a baseball bat at her side and a cup on the table, for her daughter to come home. Miss Piggy's sister took the bat away right as he came in, but his mom threw the cup and hit Miss Piggy on the head so hard that he fell down. Then my mom hurried all of us out of the room.

There was one time that he promised himself that he would dress as a girl: on the day of his mother's funeral. Everybody was doubting him because he never wanted to change how he dressed. Even on Halloween, he doesn't want to change back into a girl. During the funeral, we were waiting for her to come out of the house, but she didn't. And then she did. She was in a girl's dress and she was crying. She looked like a man in drag. She was the main one crying when everyone lined up at the casket to say goodbye. After the funeral was over, and her mother was in the hole in the ground, Miss Piggy changed back into his regular clothes; his pants were sagging, his hair was slicked back, his leg hair was showing, his shirt was so big you couldn't see his breasts. And he was happy.

The Man with the Straight Face

by ANA ENCISO

Age 15, Balboa High School

The man with the straight face
only smiles on occasion;
He only laughs at certain times.
The expression on his face:
dimples, butt-chin, wide smile that wrinkles his cheeks,
and teeth not white nor yellow but somewhere in
    between.
Glossy, droopy eyes that make him look forever sad.
Hair so thin he can barely brush it because he'll go bald,
yet still hard to keep in control.
He had no discipline, but always drank,
like his dad and most of his brothers before him.
He started when I was three,
and by the time I was seven, we all knew.
Almost every night he went out to the bar.
I have memories of being scared
of the possible fight
or car accident,

or arrest.
When he left he'd be gone for hours;
sometimes he didn't even come home.
When he did return he'd want to talk about almost
    everything:
all the girls he used to have when he was younger
and how much things had changed.
I think that was one of the reasons he loved the bar:
his well-known skills at the pool table.
He had all these trophies he kept,
he brought home one almost every other year
'93, '95, '97, '99, '00, '01, '03.
If he wasn't talking about the girls he'd had or the tro-
    phies he'd received,
He would say
no matter what we did, stupid or not,
he'd always love us,
no matter why we left,
or how long we were gone,
we could always come home.
One time,
I don't even know how,
he ended up on our kitchen floor
pretending to be swimming,
moving his arms and legs and everything,
but instead of holding his breath
he was laughing non-stop.
My mom standing next to us, me and my sister, mad
like usual.

He looks at us with those glossy, droopy eyes
making it seem as if he is forever sad and always crying.
That smile—fake but true—
that looks like he really doesn't want to smile.
Just in those features I can tell he really loves us
even if it's just a little that he cares.
(Well if he didn't, after at least ten years
and four girlfriends on the side,
why would he still be here?)
Most of all I can't forget my tenth birthday,
when he thought I was eight;
he forgot those two years when he was gone.
No matter what he does or doesn't do,
if he lies, or forgets to do something,
like forgetting to pick me up after school,
I can't help but not be mad at him.
No matter where we live,
if it's a car or a two-bedroom house for five people,
living with my dad will be like living in a palace.
Getting almost all I want,
if not something to replace it.

Obituary in Three Drafts

by TERESA COTSIRILOS

Age 17, College Preparatory High School

*T*o the editor: please include the following in the obituary section of tomorrow's paper —E.P.

PEDERSON-POLK, Christopher, left us on
January 12, 2005, in Berkeley at age 41. Until the tragic accident that caused his passing, Christopher was full of love and
life in the face of struggle. He was fascinated by trees. Even as
a child we collected leaves from the sycamore tree, the one on the
lawn of the concave house. He'd turned it into a game, pretending
he could stop whenever he wanted, and whoever picked up the
most leaves won. At the time I had ten stitches in my head from
trying to be like Chris. We talked about kindergarten, farting, and
who passed the doozies, and sometimes he gave me extra leaves so
I would win. Then Chris put the leaves in plastic bags and saved
them in a box. I don't know why I remember this.

Pederson-Polk, who is survived by his brother Ethan, was
a native of San Leandro, but he ran away from home three times
when we were kids because he knew the UPS men were trying to
kill him. It hadn't always been this way. The UPS man who always

delivered our packages was a regional poker champion named Gene, and whenever he stopped at our house Chris and I would beg him to tell us *again* about that time he anteed up with his thumb in Vegas. Then one April, Gene delivered Chris' birthday presents, and Chris hid in the closet with a baseball bat.

What happened wasn't my fault, even though everyone will say it is. Chris had to take responsibility for himself. I had to stop being the enabler and let him deal with the consequences.

Services will be held on Saturday, January 15, at Epworth Methodist Church in Berkeley. He slept in the basement there several times in the past year. He was kicked out each time because he stole all the church bulletins and turned them into origami pigs. He always took the damned leaves with him.

To the editor: please include the following in the obituary section of tomorrow's paper —E.P.

PEDERSON-POLK, Christopher, died on January 12, 2005, at the age of 41. Those fortunate enough to know him admired him for the resiliency he displayed throughout his struggles. A native of San Leandro, he ran away three times because of the UPS men, but I always knew he'd come back home because of the leaves. That crazy guy, the guys at school would say. They stole his box that time and spilled all the leaves into the gutter, and Chris howled and fell to his hands and knees, digging the leaves back out. I broke Erik Lytle's nose during Knock-Out at recess, in front of a girl he liked, and they never bothered Chris again. A family moved into the concave house and told him to stay away from their sycamore tree. He came at night to get the leaves instead. They put up a fence. He was arrested for trespassing the next day.

"Don't tell UPS I'm here," he always said. "Please, I'll leave as soon as I can, really. I'm just here for the leaves."

A week ago today I'd heard he was living in an apartment in East Oakland, and I took the day off from work. There was broken glass on the street in front, and a man who said he was John the Baptist asked me for change. Chris had left his door unlocked. The stench of urine, grunge, and fresh decay was heavy in the dark. The floor was carpeted with powdered sugar, just like the last place he'd had. Phalanxes of ants and roaches plowed through the sugar, leaving tire tracks behind. "Jesus," I said.

"Don't talk so loud," said Chris, and I made out the glint of his eyes in the dark. He was crouched naked in a corner, holding his head in his hands. He had carefully positioned himself in an oval of bare floor so that his body didn't touch any of the sugar. "You'll wake up Clark Gable," he said.

"You've been shooting up again, haven't you?"

"Don't wake him up!"

"Look at you; would you take a look at yourself?"

"They sent you, didn't they?" he said. "You're trying to kill me again, aren't you?"

"Jesus, put some clothes on—"

"Get it over with, will you? Tell UPS to go screw themselves after you're done with me!"

"Put some clothes on!" I waded through the sugar to the bathroom. I was wearing my second-best suit, and it was so rancid then that I was scared to take it to the cleaners. They might ask for an explanation. "Come on," I said. "You'll feel better if you take a shower—"

"No, no, don't! You can't go in there!"

"Take a *shower.*"

"He lives in there, don't wake him up!" he screamed. "You've come to wake up Clark Gable, you're coming to kill me. Oh God, you're coming to kill me!"

"No one's coming to—look, maybe we should go to that center again, the one with the hula dancer in the fish tank. You liked that, didn't you?" Chris sobbed dryly and hid his face against the wall. "Didn't you? I'm telling you, you liked Dr. Zltowsky. Remember him?"

"Hornets came out," Chris muttered.

"What?"

"He opened his mouth and the hornets came out, okay? They came out!"

"Oh, god." I ran my fingers through my hair. "You seriously need medication."

"I take medication," Chris said, wiping the sweat from his face.

"No, you crazy guy, you shoot up."

"Are you trying to keep me from being happy? You're all just trying to keep me from being happy!"

"Just get in the shower," I said. "I used up a sick day for this."

"Ethan," he said, and forced a smile. He'd lost three teeth since I'd last seen him. "Ethan, it's *me*, you wouldn't do this to *me*. Would you?"

I pinched the bridge of my nose and closed my eyes. "Get in the shower."

"No, no, please—"

"You know, this is crazy."

"I'll give you my leaves," Chris said.

"Just think, would you? Just—I know you know there's nothing in there!"

"I'll do anything for UPS, anything—"

"There's nothing there, just—look!" And I opened the door. I wanted him to ask me for help, just so I could tell him no, but he lay there howling, curled up like an armadillo with his eyes closed and his head thrown back. I left. He had to take responsibility for himself. I had to stop being the enabler. Sometimes it takes hitting rock bottom to change.

Services will be held on Saturday, January 15, at—

I wish I'd been the one to jump in front of a train at the Ashby Station. Then he'd have to be alive. He'd be chatting to a pretty girl in a coffee shop and think *she has no idea my brother killed himself, I'm sipping my coffee and talking about gas prices like my brother didn't kill himself. She has no idea something's wrong.* He'd be afraid to go to sleep every night of his goddamn life, dodging the insomnia and epileptic dark—ensnared in what I'd done.

To the editor: please include the following in the obituary section of tomorrow's paper —E.P.

PEDERSON-POLK, Christopher, passed on January 12, 2005, at the age of 41. He is survived by his brother Ethan. Services will be held on Saturday, January 15, at 3:30, at Epworth Methodist Church. May those who deserve peace find it.

Chaparrito Pero Picoso

by FREDY CORONADO

Age 17, Balboa High School

I am so short and I feel
like a dwarf.
My size is 5′3″.
I want to be 5′6″—
taller
than I am now.
I wanna touch the
ceiling
with my hands
but I use my imagination
and I touch
the sky.
I can't jump
high
but I can run fast.
I fit anywhere
but I can't reach everything.
I am a shorty guy

with giant feelings.
I know
everything looks different
for me.
When I wake up in the morning
I'll catch my face straight on
in the mirror
and I
start thinking each day
will be better.
I am
as I am,
as my friends say,
chaparrito pero picoso,
and I
feel good
because I know
that I have many, many
friends on my side.
The best thing is
I know
that I will always be the same:
chaparrito pero picoso-
short but spicy.

Escape

by JESSICA BALIDIO
Age 16, Balboa High School

Standing there waiting to board,
terrified,
I want to call him and say goodbye.
I try to escape for a moment to walk to the pay phones.
All the chaos with the crowded seating doesn't allow me
to break away.
Hot chocolate just the way I like it, in my hand and
ready to drink.
Not too hot and not too cold, but just right.
I see my dad walk away to have a smoke.
I know that's my chance—take it now.
I hold my little brother by the hand so he won't run off
and blame me for getting lost later.
I pick up the phone.
Dial tone.
I deposit $.50, touch the cold buttons with my pinky.
Three rings and a "Hello."
Later, I ask for him.

His sister is asking me to get her something pretty and I
tell her, "Okay," so she'll give the
phone to her brother.
I hear a sad, "Hello?"
We say our goodbyes and promise to stay the same.
Then an "I love you,"
and click.
Tears run down my face.
The whole family is back together now.
They call our row, and we're off.

Never Close Your Eyes

by GINA CARGAS

Age 13, Convent School

I stared out of the back window, trying to block out the sounds of a siren. Lying on my back with a plastic tube up my nose, I gazed into the dreary sky. It was hard to see, my eyes squinting through a maze of thick black Muni cables and electrical wires as the sun struggled to shine through the grey fog. Vaguely, I heard the paramedic beside me swiftly list out a string of instructions to another one. I had been one of those paramedics long ago, and the one thing I had noticed was that the patients who closed their eyes always died in the end. I battled with myself, straining to keep my brown eyes wide.

I supposed it was a bit ironic that I had spent twenty-three years of my life as a paramedic, sticking IVs into peoples' arms and tubes up their noses, and here I was at the end of it, a needle inserted in my right arm. I widened my eyes.

I could remember sitting beside my mother, holding her cold hand. "Don't close your eyes," I had told her, staring down at her smooth, pale skin, my own eyes filling up with salty tears. But she had closed her eyes, and now she was long gone. The large windows at the back of the truck still showed a little through the mist, but the layers of cables and scattered rainbow-striped flags flying by told me that we hadn't even left the Castro yet, my home for thirty-six years.

I silently wondered how long these paramedics had held their jobs—if they were new enough to blame themselves for death, or experienced enough to not care anymore, or older still, disturbed and sickened by the deaths they had witnessed. I opened my mouth to ask, but only a deathly rasping cough came out as the ambulance jolted over a pothole. It dissolved into laughter. The paramedic swiveled around at my scratching cackle.

She stared, clearly startled, but I was too. She was young, much too young. I had been at least ten years older when I first took that job. As we gazed at each other—a spry young woman and a wrinkling madman—I heard a muted curse from the driver.

The paramedic snapped her head away from my gaze as the ambulance came to a halt. I tried to raise my head, but I couldn't. The young paramedic's forehead was creased, brow furrowed, the only wrinkles in her smooth face. The doors were flung open and I heard the driver's gruff voice as one paramedic tested my blood pressure.

"Damn truck broke down."

I groaned. This had happened but once in my career, the day before I retired. I broke into a short burst of laughter again. I could have done with a little less irony on the day I would probably die. Ambulance breaks on the last day of my career and the last day of my life. Perfect.

Suddenly, my cackles turned to weeping. All I could feel was a horrible pain. An awful agony tore at my weak body. I glanced out the back of the ambulance, pushing pain away as the tears fell on my cheeks. I could see the driver as clearly as my poor eyesight allowed. He was a burly man with a five o'clock shadow forming on his chin, and a baseball cap pulled low across his eyes. Behind him, I recognized a row of peach apartment buildings. We were hardly out of my neighborhood, and nowhere near the hospital.

An old blue Volvo sat, horn honking, as though that sound could move our broken vehicle. The driver turned quickly and started screaming at him—face a deep, angry red—and the man soon quieted. Through unwanted tears, I could see the whole scene out of the back of the broken ambulance. There was the angry man in the Volvo, confronted by a brawny, red-faced ambulance driver, and in the background, a tall man in a maroon Santa Clara sweatshirt doing a fairly good impression of Richard Simmons in an aerobics class. I rubbed at my eyes with feeble, cracked fingers. Soon I had the teardrops gone, but the pain in my bleeding chest would not leave so easily.

As paramedics hovered above me, I tried to forget the last time I had been in an ambulance, but the memory kept coming. Her smiling face, tears pouring down her cheeks, and her smooth, unwrinkled skin lingered before my eyes. I sighed. A dead wife's face would not comfort me, even now. I felt the chilling cold seep into me, and I shivered uncontrollably. For the rest of the world, it was just another day, just another foggy San Francisco day, but for me it might be the final day.

If I had not been so stupid as to insist on driving until I was seventy-three, I would be happy and healthy, watching the PGA European Tour in my small but cozy apartment, rather than lying in the back of an ambulance, my treasured '65 Mustang crushed against a bus. I did not mourn for my injured body, only for my precious, ultimately shattered car. The irony was definitely still there. I could not stop shaking, could not stop shivering, even as the young paramedic covered me in an extra layer of blankets. I could hear the other read out my falling blood pressure.

I was not concerned with that. The pain was building in my chest. Don't close your eyes, I had told my mother, told my sister, and told my wife in their last moments. Don't close your eyes, I told myself, my only companions the paramedics standing far above me. But as I heard a second ambulance arrive to take me away, I did not want to go into the cold San Francisco air. As my bed was lifted outside of the vehicle, the shaking and shivering lessened. I looked into the young paramedic's face and smiled warmly at her through the pain. Never close your eyes, I thought. But I smiled at her again, and she gave me a tentative grin. I closed my eyes.

Sapiens Kingdom

by MAX MARTTILA

Age 16, Leadership High School

He lets the sink water run until the rust is washed away, and he splashes the clear cold water across his dry greasy face. He scrapes his wet skin against the towel on the floor. Tightening his pack, he bounces down the stairs. After he opens the door, he kneels down on one knee to tighten his shoelace. He's on the move.

As he walks, the night's cold crisp air brushes against his stiff dry nose and loosens his breath. He exhales with his dark eyes shut, covered by the shadow of his hood. His hands slide into his sweater's pocket. He exhales heavily so he can feel the air passing by his lips. He continues his march.

After a few blocks, he cuts a corner and strolls silently down to the bus stop. The city lights hang high in the sky, barely lighting his path in the distance.

He reaches the windowed shelter, and needs not wait long before the bus reaches his sight. As it screeches to a sudden halt, he steps on it and lets his pocket-change drop out of his left hand into the humming machine. He slips by the elderly couple in the front and proceeds to the back of the bus. The bus kicks up with lively movements as he drops into the back right corner seat, leaning his head against the cold window. As the bus creeps down the street, he sees few people still wandering the streets, some with a place to go, some not knowing who they are. Others' agendas made no change to his. They were nothing but mice scurrying through the dirt. As the bus begins its wide right turn, he pulled on the string hanging above his head. The bus stops and he makes his way towards the exit, his foot signaling the release of the twin doors. He is once again given away to the night.

There in front of him, he sees her. She's leaning against the crumbling tile wall of the drug store, next to the telephone off the hook. She's going at her nails. He lets go of a deep breath to catch her attention. She responds by looking up and sending him a faint smile. He returns the favor with his.

She's been waiting for him. She zips up her sweater and bends down to pick up her grey canvas carry bag. She comes up and tosses her bag over her shoulder, her eyes once again meeting his. Without a word they pick up and move, walking closely down the street away from the store. As the bus passes by them, she pops the top off of a water bottle and takes a quick sip. She passes it to him, and he too hydrates his throat with the water. He closes it and passes it back to her, and she secures it deep into her bag.

The streets they walk are almost deserted. Cars are parked all along the side of the road, but none contain any human life. Most of the shop lights are off; tall gates encase the shop's windows. As they walk alongside each other, she looks down to the concrete floor and he looks up into midnight's sky. She fastens the strap on her bag, and he glances at her black-and-white Converses. Her eyes catch his, and he retreats from her shoes and reverts his attention back to the sky above. Her hand slips into her back pocket and she retrieves a small colored sticker. She removes its adhesive back and her gentle hand slides it against a tall street pole outside of the laundromat. He grins.

They make their way down the colorfully broken street to the subway station. The stairs leading under the concrete surface lead to another, underground world of movement and blank faces. The tile walls inside are a cold white that in a way seem to support the silence. There are not many people in the station at this time, and the only sound you can hear is the constant hum of the trains. He purchases a ticket through the machine, and she pushes herself over the gate as he inserts his ticket to walk through. The cold, hard steel escalator brings them deeper, to the platforms. Sleeping at the side of the escalator is a dark snoring man, which triggers him to think about why someone would pay to sleep somewhere that wasn't that much warmer than the surface. Maybe it wasn't the warmth. Maybe it was the comforting abandonment of the surface's hard reality.

Four minutes later the train arrives and the two of them walk into its warmth, which seems to embrace them with open arms. He walks to the back of the train and she follows. They sit across from each other while the train launches into the dark abyss of tunnels. He watches the passing lights in the tunnel, and she looks down to her shoes. She looks up so often in hope of catching his eyes, but he keeps his eyes on the outside, fixated and thoughtful. Her hands hide under the sweater's sleeves and tighten her hood while she slides back deeper in the seat. Two stops later they step out of the train and out into another station.

They are now on the deep left side of downtown, closer to the industrial buildings and the dirty piers. The skies are still lit up the by city, but it is a darker light here. Halfway down the first block, she walks into a liquor store. He goes to the side of the building and, with the quickest of reflexes, opens his pack and uncaps a black can.

She comes out of the liquor store and he joins her again as they walk further down into the industrial district. Behind them they have left a simple mark of life on a dead wall. The wind is thin, but more present than before. A truck goes by and birds fly high to the top of an overhead wire. The birds sit in patience together—a rogue flock. Their wings are full, but preserved. They watch him and her.

He peers at his watch, 12:32. It doesn't matter. He is on a mission and she is just an associate. Tonight he will conquer. Tonight is his.

They cut under the freeway above, through the home of a few that could be described as the epitome of dirty. Shopping carts are tipped on their sides; ripped sleeping bags are pushed against overpass pillars and burning garbage cans. She hates it, and starts to walk faster. She can feel the faces eyeing her down, judging her for being better off. They are obviously struggling and homeless, but they have no right to judge her. She hates them. She feels relieved when they are out of the filth.

There in front of them stands their destination, a long bare building with a loading dock in front with two big driverless trucks. They scurry over to the concrete platform and he pushes a pair of small crates against the back of the truck leaning into the platform. He goes first up to the top of the truck, and she follows. From the top of the truck, he lifts himself up to the roof. She struggles a bit but makes it up. She follows him across the side of the rough black roof to the wide billboard sitting at the end of the roof. The ladder hung not too far from the ground, and he helps her up before himself.

Once they get to the top, he is already pulling cans out of his pack. He didn't sketch; he had it down. After he has a few white and black cans out, he retrieves a double layered dust mask, and a disc player. Then he is in.

He's overtaken by the disembodied voice that is the music. Its flow allows his flow, it fuels the smooth slick slide of the can up and through the white base coat that he's already left. The base coat is just the soil for the seed he is planting. The thick black lines his can spits are of such rich fruitful quality. The volume is locked at a low volume, so that he can still hear his surroundings well, but there's still enough sound to inspire his progression, to keep him going.

She sits alone at the end of the skinny billboard platform. She looks down to the road below them, bare and empty. She looks straight ahead to the freeway, cars zooming by with their own destinations.

He never did like the smell of spray paint. It always had that smell that he found to be unnecessary. But its raw appearance never lets him down. When done right, it comes out so clean and gripping, as though it hadn't been done by some mere human being. It wasn't an escape from reality; it was a piece of unreality jammed into reality's space.

As he throws on his finishing outline in white, she stands up and skips across the skinny platform next to him. He looks over to her, and then returns to his fine tuning. Once he is done, he puts the empty cans back into his bag and they crawl back down the ladder, across the roof, and down the truck and the crate.

It must be much later by now, an estimated two-thirty by her guess. They wait by a bus stop about a quarter mile away from the roof they were just on. She is cold. She is standing up, and he sits on the sidewalk. She sits next to him hoping to feel a bit more warmth. She sits close, close enough that their thighs almost meet.

He doesn't think much of her thigh next to his. After all, they are only sitting on the sidewalk. He closes his eyes and sighs. A few minutes later, the bus comes and they step on through the back door. It is empty. The bus driver doesn't yell at them for not paying, probably because it is so late.

She sits next to him again. He sits next to the window. Slowly the bus starts up and moves down the avenue and onto a freeway onramp. They pass the billboard he has just painted, and he smiles. 2:DEPHi reads across the billboard in smooth pearl-white and black outlines and shading. It is a complex net of letters that can be appreciated by those with a similar art appreciation as his. It is almost a worldwide inside club he is a part of, a subculture in which he lives. He needs no name, for his work is his name. He makes a name through his skillfully executed works. That is all he really cared about.

She looks up at him staring out the window. She knows he loves his work, but sometimes he gets too into it. She knows he can't always accept the world and the people around him. She sees a lot of good in him, but notices his weaknesses and flaws from time to time. She notices many people's weaknesses and flaws, even her own. Some people think too deeply, and she has gone deep enough, to the bottom of the abyss and back, more than once. She isn't religious, an atheist by choice. She thinks religious people were somewhat foolish and that they can't accept the reality of death and the process of evolution. Maybe there is some kind of higher power above our lives, but she sure isn't going to waste her life trying to find it. If it is an entity of love and care, it sure wouldn't want her to waste her life worshipping it. She lives freely. She gently bends her head to rest on his shoulder and closes her eyes. He feels her head rest upon his shoulder and in a way it gave him a certain sense of comfort. She really is more than just a simple acquaintance. Not necessarily a lover, more of a friend. Yeah, a friend, he thinks.

The bus slows down as it turns off of the freeway exit and into the brightly lit downtown area. She takes her head off of his shoulder to look out the window at all the neon signs and the stores and huge skyscrapers. She sometimes feels intimidated by the enormous size and intensity of the city, but it still has that sense of home. It is a home where not everything has been seen, a home of many people. She doesn't see them all as complete strangers, but more as people she just doesn't know. She knows he doesn't feel the same. He must not feel intimidated by the city. He must feel above it.

They get off the bus and step onto the brick sidewalk. He doesn't know why the city has spent so much money to put brick into the sidewalk, and neither does she. They could use all that money to help all the homeless people that fill the streets. The sky above seems so far away to her. Buildings stand at ground level but look down on her from hundreds of feet up. They are second to the clouds. Many are sheltered in grids of glass that reflect the dark illuminated sky above. She wishes that one day she can go up that high and stand between the buildings and the sky. That would lift her spirits high, just to shout out to the world below, and to feel on top.

The traffic lights are so bright. The red and green lights hold a bright color that he wishes to control. He wishes that he could put something that bright on a wall without permission. He wishes that he could be the one to grab eyes with light that could flow along with the color and the shape that he has already wielded as a weapon. Yes, it was a weapon. A weapon that slays those who own huge property and use it only for the good of their own selfish profitable cause, not for the good of humanity—his weapon, stolen from the rich and given to the poor. In this day and age the world is filled with advertisements for things that people really don't need. So many people waste their entire lives to make money. Money is nothing. Money is just paper, just green paper. Art is worth so much more. Love is worth so much more. Happiness is worth so much more. Life is worth so much more.

They keep their steps steady down the brick sidewalks. A small flock of pigeons flies above them. She watches the flock, as does he. The flock watches them as well. She feels tired. Their pace is slowing. Without a hint, he pulls a small fat black marker out of his pack, and quickly writes *2:dephi* on a glass bus shelter. The marker goes back into his backpack as fast as it came out. The pigeons see the thick black ink drip down the glass.

The night is still young in his mind. There is still so much that can be done. But he too feels somewhat tired. The night's activities have left him with a sense of content. He is pleased, but oddly enough wishes she could be as well. She spends so much time with him, and yet she doesn't look very satisfied by the night's activities. He just doesn't know what to do. Although his skills in self expression are so strong in so many mediums, his social tendencies that deal with self expression from one human being to another in one-on-one conversation is limited. He'd rather hide it in some kind of production. Expressing feelings and thoughts through other ways feels out of the ordinary for him.

She turns into the big hotel with its red velvet carpet. He follows, not knowing where she is leading him. She turns two corners and comes to an elevator door at the end of the lobby hall. Soon after she presses the button, the doors open and they step inside. It takes them to the 34th floor and they step off. She looks over at him and smiles. He tries his best to give a smile that will make her think he knows where she is going, but he knows she knows, so he just lets out a faint laugh.

After a silent walk down the hall she pushes open a heavy door and goes through another. Behind another corner is a staircase, and she quickly steps up. She pushes open a final door at the top of the stairs, and he can see the illuminated sky above. They are on the roof.

As the door shuts slowly behind them, she walks a small circle, looking up all of the while. A series of concrete ledges sits in the middle of the roof, and she sits on one. He joins her.

She lets out a sigh of relief. It must be at least four o'clock, but it still doesn't matter. Once again she lets her head rest on his left shoulder. Then her hand slowly touches his, and they interlock. She moves up to whisper something into his ear, and he kisses her cheek.

Quiet

by HUA LING ZHAO

Age 15, Galileo Academy of Science & Technology

Lips tie together
It's the end of earth
Healthy tanned little hands
Praying and wondering
Buffalo eyes wide open
The blank quiet face
Yet a volcano about to explode
Good bye Dad, rest in paradise

Boy Up a Tree

by ELIZABETH NEVEU

Age 18, home schooled

He can see me. Though the eyes he cut in his paper mask are a finger-width too far apart.

As I stare I realize what he reminds me of: a koala—comfortable, relaxed, wrapped around a trunk fifteen feet up in the air. The scenery, far from a eucalyptus grove in Australia, is a bleak courtyard of beaten brick apartments and dirt. His tree stands alone as bare as its surroundings, all its limbs missing but one. Somehow, though he can't touch one hand to the other, he is even with a second story window. He looks down at me and I am jealous. This boy, seven years alive, is omnipotent. Through the holes in that mask he sees things not as they are but as what he could make them. The air in this hard, bland, empty space is mixed with the haze of his thoughts. It gathers in shapes and forms I can't see, and seeps into the tired old buildings and softens them to clay. He looks down at me, and I feel foreign. I try to remember what it was like, before my imagination had congealed.

Pink

by DANIEL ABELLA

Age 16, Leadership High School

The moonlight shone greatly onto the green field that laid in front of my vision. The green grass looked a little more defined in the full moon. I stood on the dike that overlooked the field and it looked as if it were an endless forest that led into the abyss that lay at the end of the road. The tears from God fell upon the earth and mixed subtly into the great ground He Himself made. I kneeled down and reached in for a handful of the ground. As it gathered into my palm I felt its pain. I looked at my Rolex watch. It read 2:15 AM on June 25th. I had fifteen more minutes until I was to finish my assignment. I felt the weariness of the job through my old bones and through my soul.

My soul was a funny concept. I was never blessed with one or even a conscience, but I felt them in my older decades. Nightly and daily I hade to come to secluded corners of the world to do the duty my father passed onto me as he lay in his chambers retiring from this job. The piercing duty of a drop-dead mercenary ran through me every time I came on one of my jobs. I hated these assignments the most. The little ones, they seemed to be the most difficult and most demanding ones.

A red rose stood on the top of the hill, surrounded by many sunflowers and weeds that stood up with ugly beauty. It was like seeing a beautiful woman with skin so lavish and eyes so big and bright standing alone surrounded by hunchbacked men with ripped faces and torn souls. Scorn for life, I was. As a child I grew and admired those who were able to become angelic figures and mystic guardians while I became the mysterious hurt and pain of inevitability. I took out a cigar that I had been saving for the most vigorous of tasks tonight, this was it. It was Cuban. Its blunt edge engulfed in my purple lips, I lit it up with my golden Zippo. Its flame gave birth to a bright light that illuminated the whole circumference of the hill. It also hit my face, which felt so good.

I hadn't been in the sunlight for the past week and a half. It felt like it had been a lifetime, and for some it had. As I lit the cigar I kneeled again and ripped the rose from its mother and gazed at it. It was ripe and red, I had not seen something so red and beautiful in years. It was destiny for me to see this rose, as everything was. However, like all things, the rose lost its red color and turned into a pale grey like sitcoms from the 1950s. The petals kept on peeling but soon enough the flower became ash and blew away in the Oklahoma winds. I dropped the stem and looked into the winds and saw bits of ash washing away in the night sky. Everything I touched turned to ash and swept away into the nothingness of the night. I hated the night.

I walked down the dike and into the green fields that stood in front of me and the assignment. I slowly strutted through the field and watched as every piece of green grass and the long wheat stems that touched me wither as the rose did. A memory, flying away in the night because it became hollow ash. I continued to smoke my cigar as I came ever so close. I exhaled with extreme force and anger because I hated this job. I hated being the exact opposite of the King Midas. I turned things to ash and dirt. But I was born into this life—I didn't ask for it.

I inched closer to my destination and finished my cigar. I dropped it into a garbage can that stood on the outskirts of the wheat fields and looked at the golden watch that stood still on my wrist. It read 2:26 AM. I began to gallop a bit towards the porch of the Holt home. It was a wooden home made entirely of logs and tar. The home was dark and broken down, it had a bird feeder and a dirt road leading to it. I would have taken the dirt road, but a tractor stood in the way as if it were some sort of gate leading into a palace. The palace was home to the Holt family.

The Holts were a family that had been on the downfall ever since Joe Holt (the father) went to jail for manslaughter. I would be visiting him in three days. I knew Angola prison ever so well. I had been there nearly five times a year for the past ten years. I used to be fearful of going to jails. Prisoners become much better at seeing and can see me and the dead coming even before I know I am going to make an appearance.

I took the key that was on the top of the door seal, no one knew about the key except me and the family members. I pushed the key into the door knob; it opened quickly. All doors knew me and the hands I had. I twisted the knob open and walked into the entrance hall of the secluded home. A "Bless this Home" sign stood next to a crucifix on the north wall with a coat rack and small table that was made out of glass. A staircase stood next to that and creaked loudly. I, however, never made noise on the creaky stairs I visited nearly every week. As I climbed up the steep stairs I felt my non-existent heart beat like the helicopter did earlier at the hospital I visited for Jenny Clarke, or the one I visited yesterday for Greg Richards III. I hated the sound of blades chopping into the air as if the air had done something to the earth.

I slowly opened the first door on the left, and in it was four pink walls with pictures of Dora the Explorer and Disneyland. I felt the urge to cry knowing what I was about to do, I felt like a monster. I looked up at the ceiling aiming for the face of God and was angry, I knew it was his will that I did this and that I do it at 2:31 exactly, but I felt like jumping into the pits of hell before I doing this. I knew hell; I had been there to drop off deliveries before. It was a room with four endless white walls and everyone had their mouths and ears sewed tightly so you could not speak or hear, demons prancing around and beating those who prayed silently to the One who sat on his throne in heaven. I had feared being there for more then five minutes—five minutes felt like an eternity.

It was 2:30, and I walked towards the bed and looked at the angelic figure that dreamed of queenhood and ponies. I hated doing this, but I knew she would be spared the heartache that is growing up, especially the fact that if she were to live she would live and die in Oklahoma and never leave the town she had already began to dream of leaving. She was queen Jody in her dreams and in her imagination that had her spinning in the clouds with her three dead brothers and her father who she thought had died in the real world. Not the case. I looked at the mirror that hung on the wall and saw my face, the face of death. I straightened my tie and cleaned off my suit. I bent down to the height of her bed and blew a gust of wind in her ear. It woke her up upon feeling.

She looked at me, not fearing what was to come because this child did not know who I was. My face looked like that of her father. She could not tell that I was not her father in this moonlight, which usually told all stories sure and true. She had dark eyes, not darker than mine, but they were still able to drown me upon sight. I really wished I wasn't here, but the truth was I had to be. I was obligated. She smiled and before she had the chance to say a work I motioned her to be quiet.

"Hi." I said. I smiled and she looked into my smile and knew it wasn't all there. She thought she was dreaming so she didn't use her usually sharp wit to call me on the fake smile.

"Hello." She was five. I saw her soul, true and pure, though her brown eyes that glowed in the night mist of Oklahoma.

"Are you ready for a trip?" I knew that if she thought this was not a dream she would have yelled for her mother, which would have been to no avail because I was the night mist no one saw unless they needed to see me.

"Where are we going?" She was happy because her improvised neighborhood was the only place her, her mom, and her older sister saw. Her sister would leave with her mom after this night to Washington, D.C. Her sister would become a congresswoman and her mom would write a novel.

"Somewhere that you can play with ponies and clouds everyday, forever. To the castle that is pink and full of your brothers and their happiness, and yours too. To the place that you've dreamed of for a long time." I said, I began to feel a wet drop fall from my eye. Had this girl continued on she would have fallen from grace and into the wheat field to die a lonely death.

"Okay!" She said excitedly. I grabbed her hand from under the pillow and bent down to kiss her forehead. She went limp, her eyes shut and along with it her soul. I took a strand of light from her tear duct and laid it onto the floor where it morphed into a transparent version of little Kate Holt in her pink pajamas and her toe socks, with teddy in her left hand. I grabbed her hand and walked her down the hall and down the stairs to a glowing light.

The light was only an outline of the door that held her final stop on its other side, five years old and standing on heaven's doorstep. I opened the golden door and the blinding light came into sight. The purplish pink clouds greeted us and in the horizon the pink castle stood with a hot pink flag atop. She ran towards it before her unicorn jumped her onto its back and galloped its way towards the horizon. I reached for my breast pocket and looked at the white piece of paper with today's names.

~~James Henderson~~
~~Jenny Clarke~~
~~Mimi James~~
~~Kate Holt~~
Thomas Christian

You Bring the Muy Caliente Outta Me

by MAYRA RECINOS

Age 15, Balboa High School

You bring the taquerias outta me.
The burrito and quesadilla lover in me.
The *arroz y frijoles* eater outta me.
The *novela's* on tonight outta me.
Proud to be Latina.
Yup... that's what you get outta me.

You bring the Latin Lover outta me.
Let my hair *suelto,*
Flor en el pelo outta me.
The Salsa, Merengue, and Flamenco dancer
    outta me.
Me encanta sentir the music.
The Spanish knee-to-ankle dress *cuando bailo,*
    "Oye Como Va" outta me.

How do you bring the naturalness outta me?
'Cause I tend to overpluck my eyebrows

To where you can't see them anymore.
Mask my neutral lips with red or brown,
And trace my eyes so black, that it becomes
    repelling.
To the point where you don't wanna take me
    out
'Cause you don't want to be singled out in
    a crowd.

You bring the "Let's Get Loud" outta me.
I'm like a *cholita* when it comes to you.
Who is she to you??
Or...
Que me miras, guey?
Overprotective like you're cheating with *esa estu-*
    pida chica next door.
I need to cool off *como esas* out-of-the-oven
    enchiladas.
Because you claim I do *too* much.
Y que tiene?

You bring *lo mejor* outta me.
Don't expect the best and don't expect *lo peor*.
Tryna be *coqueta* with those *minifaldas*,
Even though I know I don't gotta try hard!
Whether I'm wearing a big ol' t-shirt and
    sweats,
Or a little *blusa* with tight, low-rise jeans...
You somehow bring the *muy caliente* outta me.

Insomnia

by JOANNA AMICK

Age 14, City Arts and Technology

I can't sleep. It's just like waiting for your death in a prison cell. Being tortured each day, only the reward for suffering is sleep, not death. I sit here on my computer knowing that I will be doing nothing for an hour. No one gets up till six. I have time to ponder life. I hear the dog run by and I finally notice the light in the hall is on. Maybe people are awake, maybe I don't have time to ponder. My stomach churns as it waits for food. Being randomly stabbed by the invisible knife, I ache. My head hurts, my stomach hurts, my legs hurt. All I want to do is sleep.

Insomnia is a curse. I do like to stay up till the early hours of the morning but I still like to sleep. My eyes won't close and my mind won't clear. I keep tossing and turning. Books going through my head. It's too hot. I throw off the blanket, leaving me with only my pajamas and sheet covering me. I shift so that my legs are over the sheet. Still too hot. I turn off the nearby light. Darkness swallows me. It's as dark as the jungle nights. The trees covering up the moonlight the same way the door and the curtains hide the dawn.

I hear the doors open and close, the faucets turing on. They are up early today. Maybe I should stop and go back in bed? But it won't do. My eyes are glued open yet burn to be sewn shut. The fan blows a breeze on me. It's refreshing. It feels a lot better than the salty, sticky ocean air coming from the beach that is not even a mile away. The air from the fan moves away, leaving me trying to cool down between its occasional visits.

I'm thinking of what today will be like. My last day to be on the Hampton beach. Feeling slightly sick to my stomach, I begin to think of the long day ahead. Monday pops into my mind. I should start packing today, for tomorrow, I'll be going home at 2 PM. I'll be alone for the rest of the day. But not long. My heart is pumping. Thoughts of someone coming through the bedroom door startle me. Will they know I was up all night? But I wonder why I worry. I wonder why I bother typing this. I realize why: I'm passing the time. Altough it is still moving slowly it is better than lying awake on a warm mattress with an even warmer pillow next to my blushing cheek. Tossing and turning every minute—every second—and not knowing what time it is.

I realize that is one of the flaws of the house: The clocks are in the living room, except for the clocks on the computers. I look down at the floor near the screen door and see that under the curtains there is sunlight. It is now 5:37. Dawn. Day has come and night has gone. Sleepiness is filling up inside me like a bath tub that was left with the water running all night. Soon it'll all vanish down the drain just like my exhausted feeling will. I'll be awake and alive and I will spend my last day on the Hampton beach for this summer.

Piratehood Explained

by LAYLA DURRANI
Age 14, Hoover Middle School

To be a pirate, you need to do more than put on a plumed hat and say "Aaarrgh!" every moment you get. It means you have to feel a situation with your fingertips. You must have conversations with seagulls, find out about the sweet smell of the nests from which they learned to fly. Let the ship talk to you, too. When its deck gets encrusted with brine, its pillars soggy, feel for it, caress it, kiss it with your rags and soap. Learn to smell its satisfaction after being cleaned. Smell the sea, the seaweed, the sky, the fresh smell of rain on your sails, or the swish of silk scarves and sultans' cakes. Learn to live the lifestyle, not in a career sort of way, but through your taste of sea air and the sound of far-away seahorses.

THE STORE AT 826 VALENCIA
Bring your own citrus.

THE STORE
at 826 VALENCIA

"Definitely one of the top five pirate stores I've been to recently."

—DAVID BYRNE

What happens at the Store at 826 Valencia? Many have said that upon entering San Francisco's only independent pirate supply store, they get a sensation of déjà vu. Others walk in and feel at once the miracle work of an unseen hand. And there are those whose eyes bulge and shrink simultaneously, their thoughts so convoluted they are unable to shout or mutter the question that most plagues them: "What is this place?"

Top Ten T-Shirts
Our Customers Have Worn

1. Bass Fishing: An American tradition since 1801

2. C'est Superb! Rainbow Airlines

3. I [heart] math

4. I got 80 million for my venture capital firm and all I got was this lousy T-shirt.

5. There is nothing lucky about a bunny with no feet.

6. Stanford Blood Center

7. Saddle Up, Ride 'Em

8. Shaolin Fighting, Confusion Fighting, Confusion Hill

9. [picture of Darth Vader pruning a hedge]

10. [picture of a parsnip]

Top Ten Things
Our Customers Have Done

1. Bartered for lard by breathing fire

2. Carried on a conversation about the mashed potatoes of their youth

3. Discussed the phrase "rotating flagellum"

4. Given us a lesson in Bahasa Indonesian while buying a buckle.

5. Introduced us to a stuffed seal named "Rachel"

6. Told us being mopped reminded them of their bat mitzvah

7. Claimed to have "a penchant for drawing cheese"

8. Used our sealing wax to make a reliquary for a departed terrier

9. Walked in carrying Wiffle balls

10. Purchased gold teeth for their entire immediate family

Top Thing Our Customers Should Not Have Done

Store Log

8/27/06

"Today I have Japanese, Chinese, and English Grammar class. I should be at my grandmother's funeral. Instead I am in the pirate store. Life is good."

Lard Log, Summer 2006

Our lard has different moods from day to day in response to the air in the Mission District. We have found that these moods can often be summed up by review quotes on the covers of works of modern fiction.

6/8/06	7/17/06
Brooding	Crisp
6/11/06	7/19/06
Unyielding	Buoyant
7/22/06	8/10/06
Gassy	Bighearted

Funny Jokes

Children in the store often try to barter for their treasure with jokes. They often do not succeed for the following reasons:

1. We have heard a lot of jokes.
2. We are skeptical of jokes involving knocking or road-crossing.
3. We don't have a very good sense of humor.

But here are some that made our lips twitch:

Q: What goes 99-clunk, 99-clunk, 99-clunk?
A: A centipede with a wooden leg.

Q: Why did, why did the, um, the lantern cross the road?
A: To buy two earrings.

Q: What do you call a man stranded in the ocean with no arms and no legs?
A: Bob.

Q: Imagine you are in a metal box. How do you get out?
A: Stop imagining it

The Supplies

Glass eye starter kit

If it is your first time buying an ocular prosthetic, we recommend this starter kit, which comes complete with a handcrafted eyeball (blue, brown, and hazel available) and a very small book on its proper care and feeding.

SeaHose

As the most trusted name in protective maritime hosiery, SeaHose are guaranteed to prevent sunburn, windburn, rope-burn, shackle-burn, chapped knees, deck splinters, and "wardrobe apathy."

Hoodies

826 Valencia hoodies are like tugboats: cute from the front, intimidating from behind.

Yosh perfumes

Yosh Han has formulated a scent for every mood, including Swashbuckler and El Capitan for the gents and Buxom and Siren for the ladies.

Notebooks, inks, and quills

Our svelte notebooks and inks are made exclusively by the sveltest Italians. Our swift quills are plucked exclusively from the swiftest fowl.

★   ★   ★

Store Thanks:

We would like to thank all of the store staff, volunteers, and contributing artists for their continued support and dedication: Jon Adams, Veronica Dakota, Jessica Fleishchman, Melanie Glass, Michelle Grier, Veronica Kavass, Noah Lang, Paul Madonna, Nicki Pfaff, Lailah Robertson, Caitlin Van Dusen, Alison Wannamaker, Dan Weiss, Liz Worthy, and of course, the cast and crew of our very own very-off-Broadway production, the fish.

Store Hours:

12-6 P.M. every day
826 Valencia Street
San Francisco, CA 94110
www.826valencia.org/store

To read the store log, browse and buy the latest merchandise, visit with Karl from beyond the grave, or keep up on events happening in the store, please visit us at www.826valencia.org/store.

[*We would like to thank the following donors and community partners for their contributions to 826 Valencia.*]

Donors

Breanna Alexander, Tom and Cindy Allen, Peter Alpert and Dale Allinson, Tracy and Andy Amanino, American Express Foundation Employee Gift Matching Program, Lisa Amick, Anonymous, Andrea Arata, Megan Armstrong and Mark Kenward, Maria Baird, Margaret Ballard, Bank of America Matching Gifts, Steven Barbour, Kirsten and Michael Beckwith, Shoshana Berger, Barb Bersche, Alec and Anne Binnie, Deirdre Birmingham, Paula Andrea Blacona, Andrew Blauner, Kevin Blinkoff, Bloomers, Jeffrey Bluestone, John and Natasha Boas, David and Anne Borrelli, Allison Boswell, Laura Boxer, Belkis Boyacigiller, Samuel and Susan Britton, Philip and Michele Bronson, Brandon Broxey, C. Breck and Anne Hitz, Brian and Gwenn Childers, Jennifer Bunshoft, Buffalo Exchange, Greg and Kathleen Calegari, Gordon Cameron, Mary Canning, Jennifer Carlisle, Giles Cassels, Doris Chang in memory of Jane Han, Chapman and Associates Charitable Foundation, Wallace Cheng, Chrysopolae Foundation, Cindy and Dan Cohen, City Arts & Lectures, Claire-Laure Enterprises, Mo Clancy, Thomas Clyde, Theresa Thorn Coyle, Craigslist, Crumbs, Maria Lourdes O. Damo, Jeff and Kristen Daniel of Rock River Communications, Russel Darling, Gordon Davis, Jean D'Eliso and Adam Weiss, Daniel DiPasquo, Richard and Tamara Dishnica in memory of Charlie Wincorn, Daniel Donahoe and Kathryn Woods, The Darby Foundation, Bob and Katherine Dureault, John Durham, Daniel and Diane Durst, Joanna Davis, Dylan Todd Simonds Foundation, William Eggers, Eldorado Foundation, Electronic Arts Matching Gifts Program, Bonnie and Herb Elliott, Marie Estorge, Richard Everett, Britte-Marie Evers, Caterina Fake, Fannie Mae Foundation, Krista Farey, Robin Farley, Elizabeth Feery, Oscar Felix, Katy Filner, Elena Fischbacher, Fleishhacker Foundation, Florence Hochman, Fraenkel Gallery, Inc., Julie Franki, Sara Anne Furrer and Annette Bianchi, Jodi Gallant, Gallo Family Fund, Kat Galvan, Stuart Gansky in memory of Joseph Silver, Gap Foundation, Max Gardner, Rita Gardner, Diane Garfield, KC and Thomas Garrett, Daniela Garza, Jesse Gazzuolo, Cindy Waszak Geary, Ann Ferrer-Van Gelder, Genentech CIT Department, Camellia George and Aleksander Felstiner, Anne Germanacos, Roger and Brenda Gibson, Jennifer Gilbert and Ron Fagen, Mary Gillis and Steve Schwartz, Michael Ginther and Jim O'Donnell, Bob and Katy Glass, John and Tina Monaco Glynn, Kenneth Goldberg and Tiffany Shlain, Roger and Linda Goossens, Marguerite Grady, Brian and Susan Gray, James Grenert, Grey San Francisco, Shawn Grunberger, Kevin Guilfoile, Joe and Barbara Gurkoff, Larry and Jackie Gutsch, Natira Hammerstrom, Daniel Handler and Lisa Brown, Sharon Hanson, Claire Harrison, Ian Hart and Nick LaRocque, Ryan Harty and Julie Orringer, Ellen Hathaway, Noah Hawley, Carol Hazenfield, Jason Headley, Holly Hirshfield and the Summit Family, Kawika Holbrook, Hilary and Tom Hoynes, Deirdre and Christopher Hockett for The Hockett Family Fund, James Hsu, Wyatt Hunter, Isabel Allende Foundation, J. Glynn and Company, J.B. Berland Foundation, June Jackson, Abigail Jacobs, Barry Jacobs, Jay Jacobs and Liz Hume, Richard and Nancy Jacobs, Paul Jacobson, Ian and Gail Jardine, Jeffrey and Jeri Lynn Johnson, Jennifer Jones, Jesse Tepper Properties, Jewish Community Center of San Francisco, Melind Joseph John, David and Allyson Johnson, D.S. and Jean Johnston, Brewster Kahle and Mary Austin, Edward and Joyce Kalush, Betty Karsh, Charles Katz, Keith Knight, Keker Family Foundation, Kevin Kelly, Robert Kikuchi-Yngojo, Kimball Foundation, Meaghan Kimball, Koret Foundation, Carol Krop, Alan Mark Kudler and Linda Glick, Jordan and Tara Kurland, Margarita Bekker, Benoit Lacasse, La Fetra Foundation, Mary and Nathan Lane III, Brian Larson, Liz Jaroslow, Lasseter Family Foundation, Susan Leach, Jane Lee, John Lee, Wendy Szeto Lee and Brian D. Lee, Phred Lender, Beverly and Phil Lenihan, Frank Leonard, Seth Leonard and Matchflick.com, Shira Levine, R. Michael Lieberman and Deborah Bishop, Alvin Lin, Marc Lipsett and Elizabeth Jaroslow, Barbara Lobb, Richard and Nancy Lopes, Laura Lucs, Mike Lynch, Ann Lyons, Magowan Family Foundation, Erika Malzberg, Jonathan Marlow, Linda Marousek, James and Jean Martin, Mary A. Crocker Trust, Brian and Joanne Maude, Mary McLoughlin, Matt and Sophia Mengarelli, Sarah Minn, Maura and Robert Morey, MBG Entertainment, Inc., Keith and Elise McDonald, Steven Merrill, MetLife Foundation, Burton and Sandra Meyer, Gary Meyer, Katherine Michiels, Jann Middo, Tom Molanphy, Abner Morales, Morrison and Foerster Foundation, John and

Caryl Morrison, Muffie Meier, Norm Meyrowitz, John Muller, Michael and Gayle Murphy, Terry Myers, Catherine Nash, National Endowment for the Arts, Bita Nazarian, Chris Nelson and Amy Rees, Nickel vs. Bank of America Settlement Fund, Debra Niemann and David Brodwin, Reece Halsey North and Kimberley Cameron, Monica and Michael Norton, Tim and Ali Nufire, Jennifer Nye in memory of Patrick Tweed, Shannon O'Leary and the Mission Creek Music and Arts Festival, Kathryn Olney and Clifford Jay Bell, Thomas and Nancy O'Mara, Oppenheimer Funds Legacy Matching Gifts Program, Katy Orr, Paragon Real Estate Group of San Francisco, Jessica Partch in honor of Doug Ferguson, Lyssa Kaye Paul, Louise Paustenbach, Eugenia Payne, Peet's Coffee and Tea, Peninsula Community Foundation, Kenneth Peters, Annette Pineda, Carol and Frank Pitman, Pottruck Family Foundation, Quadra Foundation, Katherine Quigg, Alexandra Quinn, Martin and Maria Quinn, Mark Rabine, Sally Randel, Oliver Raskin, RealNetworks Foundation Matching Gifts Program, Catherine Remick, James Rocchi, Aesop Rock, Rock-a-Billy's New and Used CDs and Tapes, Brianna Rohlfs, Jonathan Root in honor of Rebecca Szeto and Roger Hagen, Dawn Ross, Betty and Tim Royce, Dorothy Ruderman, The Ruth L. Lee Fund, Lisa Ryers, Susan Sakuma, San Francisco Arts Commission, The San Francisco Foundation, Penelope Satterwhite, Anthony Saxe, Edward Saxon, Lawrence Schear, Jason Schultz, Rodney Searcey, William Schroeder, Kathryn Scott and Melanie Sherk, Lisa Sedgley, Erin Seely, Steven Seligman, Ben Shaw, Charlotte Sheedy, Melanie Sherk, Laura and Peter Shumaker in honor of Andree Abecassis, Belinda Sifford, Costanzo and Beverly Silvestre, Ryan Sims, Donald Simms, Mark and Judy Singer, Elizabeth Sittenfeld, Evan Sornstein, Nancy Spector, Keith Spicknell, Laura and Greg Spivy, Mark J. Spolyar, Starbucks Foundation, Mike and Shauna Stark, Marla and David Steuer, Steven Barclay Agency, The Stocker Foundation, Jeremy Stone and the Matz/Stone Family, Andrew Strickman, Danielle and Leonard Strickman, Greg Sumner and Anne Crosthwaite, Sydney Goldstein and Charles Breyer, Syida Long, Synergy School, Tae Kwang Kim, Janet Taylor, Tom and Susan Teel, Alex Tenorio, Thendara Foundation, M. J. Thomas, Mark Thomas and Susan Bernstein, Thrice, Anne Marie Tickner, Tin Man Fund, Jennifer Traig, Mason and Shirley Trihn, Trillium Fine Art Press, Twilight and Marc Freedman Foundation, United Way of the Bay Area, Valerie Wolfgram, Eugene and Suzanne Valla, Tony and Isabella Valli, Duane Valz, Donovan Van, van Löben Sels/Rembe Rock Foundation, Toby Verey, Paul and Inger Vida, Vista Foundation, Michael and Raynor Voorhies, Greg Wadsworth and Ann Scott, James and Karen Wagstaffe, Ayelet Waldman and Michael Chabon, John and Pamela Walker, Nina Watson, Walter and Elise Haas Fund, Wells Fargo Community Support Campaign, John Whelan, Charles and Sharon Wienbar, Denise Wilkins, Julie Willing and Timothy Doherty, Catherine Marie Willis and Peter Rowson, Richard Wilson and Christina Henry de Tessan, Stuart Wilson, Windfall Foundation, Jim and Lynne With, Rick Wolfgram, Kimberly and Martin Wong, Andrew Wylie, The Wyss Foundation, Yahoo! Corporation Donation Matching Fund, Earl Yerina, Anthony and Vivian Zaloom, Alan Zatopa, Michael Zatopa and Ellen Stephens, Robert and Anne Zerbst, Zickler Family Foundation

In Kind Donors

Lisa Amick, Another Planet, Atlas Café, Babylon Burning Screen Printing, Bevilacqua & Sons Construction, BiRite Market, Boku Books, Jotham Burrello, Capitol Electric, Case+Abst Architects, Cha Cha Cha, Chenery Park, City Lights Publishers, Clift Hotel, Commodore Hotel, Conklin Bros. Carpet/Shaw Industries, Steve Dombrowski, Domino's Pizza, Elephant Rock Productions, Genentech, Glass Scratch Removers, Golden State Carpet, Green Apple Books and Music, HarperCollins Publishers, Bill Higgins, Daniel Kaufman, Kikkerland/Moleskine, Krispy Kreme Doughnuts, Mark Krueger, John Larkin, Larratt Plumbing, Chad Lent, Marianna Leuschel, Andy Lipnick, Live Nation, Lurie Management, Maverick Restaurant, McAdams/Cage, Lucas Murgida, Katy Orr, Jeni Paltiel, Papalote, Peet's Coffee and Tea, Penguin Books, Peninsula Builders, Pixar Animation Studios, Platanos, Ravenswood Winery, Recchiuti Confections, Ritual Coffee Roasters, Roshambo Winery, Adam Salkin, Salon.com, Eva Shoshany, Swedish American Hall, Tahoe Cookie Company, Tao Café, Tartine Bakery, Tazo Tea, The Blue Plate Restaurant, The Eighth Mountain Press, Thirsty Bear Restaurant and Brewery, TicketWeb, W Hotel, Jon Wynacht, Yerba Buena Center for the Arts, Francis Yiu / Novani